The Duke's Revenge

Robyn C Rye

Published by robyncrye, 2023.

Also by Robyn C Rye

Farnsworth Sisters
Marrying a Rogue
Rescuing Hannah

The Buckingham Sisters
Lady Maggie's Challenge
Layla's Unwanted Husband

The Evans Family
Sometimes Love is not Enough
Still the One
Moving Forward

Standalone
One More Chance
Lady Jayne's Reputation
Third Time's the Charm
Can't Stop Loving You

The Marriage Scam
An Unlikely Match
Searching For You
The Unexpected Suitor
The Lady and the Duke
Starting Over
An Unforgettable Stranger
The Duke's Revenge
The Temporary Wife
Against The Odds
Betrayed
No Good Turn Goes Unpunished
Lady Eloise's Soldier
Lillian's Forbidden Beau
Remember Me
Always Second Best
When One Door Closes
Coming Home to You
Chasing Shadows
Fool Me Once
Deserting Lady Audrey
My Unlikely Saviour
Lies and Deception
A New Beginning
Julia's Second Chance
The Hidden Enemy
The Maiden's Redemption

Table of Contents

Author's message

I am an Australian author, so the spelling of some words may differ from that of the American dialect.

Thank you for joining me in telling the story of Isabelle and Zavier. I hope you enjoyed their story as much as I enjoyed recounting it.

If you enjoyed the book and have a moment to spare, I would appreciate a brief review on the page or site where you purchased the book. Reviews from readers like you make a massive difference in helping new readers find stories like The Duke's Revenge. Your help in spreading the word is appreciated.

Thank you!

Contact me at

robyncrye.author@gmail.com

Chapter One

Isabel fluttered her fan, attempting to create a breeze in the stifling room. A small smile graced her face as she listened attentively to the man seated on her left. She gritted her teeth, the slight smile never leaving her face. If there was one thing her mother had taught her, it was that a woman had to make the best match possible, and seemingly, that was the man currently boring her to tears. How many mornings must she sit here and listen to the man bragging about his possessions and wealth? Today's visit must be the tenth one Lord Raven had graced her with, and he never seemed to be trying to entertain her or further their relationship. He had gained permission from her father to court Isabelle, but they had not enjoyed carriage rides, strolls in the park, or even a walk in the gardens.

If this courtship progressed, she expected a marriage proposal. Her parents would be thrilled, as Lord Raven was wealthy and much sought after by the other debutantes. Pleasing her parents was something Isabel tried to do, but sentencing herself to a lifetime of boring monologues and sweaty hands left her feeling ill. A grimace crossed her face as the reality of a marriage to Lord Raven hit her. The eagle eyes of her mother caught the expression, and she sent Isabel a censoring glare. Lord Raven, intent on impressing Isabel with his daring feats, missed the change in her appearance. In truth, Isabel wondered if the man had looked at her at all during their afternoon tea. On the odd occasion that Isabelle roused herself to speak, Lord Raven condescendingly patted her on the hand and continued with his dialogue, completely ignoring her.

When Benz opened the door and said, "Lady Beaumont, you have another caller." Lady Beaumont raised an eyebrow at him. Isabel gave a small sigh of relief. The arrival of another caller would motivate Lord Raven to leave. Just as she hoped, Lord Raven stood and bowed over her hand and exited.

"May I call tomorrow?"

Isabelle wanted to refuse the man's request, but she knew her mother would scold her forever if she did.

When Isabelle was slow to respond, her mother spoke on her behalf.

"Certainly, Lord Raven. It would be a pleasure to see you."

Isabelle looked hopeful. "If it is fine outside, could we walk in the park or stroll in the gardens?"

"We'll see what tomorrow brings."

When the man left the room, Lady Beaumont rounded on Isabelle.

"Goodness child, what on earth made you suggest a walk in the park or a stroll in the gardens? Such forward behaviour is unbecoming."

"Mother, have you ever noticed that even though he has my Father's permission to court me, we never leave this room? It's as though he doesn't want to make our courting public. I think he's spending time with me until someone better comes along."

"Nonsense, child. He will come up to scratch; we need to be patient. Benz, are you going to show our new guest in?"

Isabelle shook her head. How long did she continue being patient when the man was not trying to take their courtship any further than the parlour? Isabelle glanced at the Benz as he hesitated. Something about their new visitor concerned him, and even though he was the consummate unflappable butler, he momentarily looked anxious.

"Certainly, my Lady." Benz stepped back from the door and intoned, "Lord Fagean, Duke of Kenmore."

Lady Beaumont shot to her feet as the man entered the room. Her response was fuelled by outrage, not admiration for the man. Isabel was astounded by her mother's unladylike behaviour, and this astonishment deepened when Lady Beaumont chose not to curtsy.

"How dare you call on us. I will have no dissolute characters like you in contact with my daughter. Your presence is unwelcome, my Lord, and I would ask you to leave."

Lord Fagean smirked. "What would you say if I asked to court your daughter?"

Isabel felt sure that her mother was on the verge of swooning. Lady Beaumont's face flushed a vivid red, and her hands fluttered in front of her. She hit the sofa with a huff. Taking matters into her own hands, Isabel rose from her seat and approached the Duke. It was an unforgivable sin to approach a man whom she hadn't met through the proper introductions, but his presence in the room overruled that piece of etiquette. With a deep curtsy, Isabel greeted the man. He was tall, and the cut of his clothes emphasised his trim torso and long legs. His dark hair was too long by conventional standards, and piercing blue eyes twinkled at her. The few grey hairs scattered through his hair attested that the Duke was older than most men looking for brides. The slight grin he gave her made her face flush.

"My Lord, please sit while I organise new refreshments."

As Isabel opened the door to give instructions to Benz, her mother rallied.

"Absolutely not, Benz. You need to escort this man from the room."

Isabel glanced at her mother and then at the face of the newcomer. Her mother's reaction to the man seemed over the top. Was there something scandalous in the man's past that her mother was privy to?

"Mother, Lord Fagean is a Duke. You can't have him escorted from the room like a criminal."

"Well, maybe not, but you, sir, can not court my daughter. We expect Lord Raven to offer for Isabel any day."

"But he has not offered yet? And is Isabel going to accept when Lord Raven offers?"

"Don't be foolish, Lord Fagean; of course, she will accept."

With a casual turn of his head, Lord Fagean scrutinised Isabel.

"And what say you, Miss Isabelle? Will you be accepting Lord Raven's offer of marriage?"

Isabelle gave a delicate shudder and said, "Not if I can help it. He is deadly boring and full of himself. I'm certain he...."

Lady Beaumont's exclamation stopped Isabelle in her tracks, and, realising what she had just divulged to a perfect stranger, she blushed furiously.

"Oh, dear. I do beg your pardon, my Lord."

"I think that settles that question. I will call for you at two, and we will announce our courtship with a drive in the park. You may bring a chaperone; no need to let the gossips have too much to talk about."

With a courtly bow to Isabelle, Lord Fagean quit the room. Isabelle fanned her face. Moments ago, Lord Fagean had filled the room with energy and purpose, and now his departure left the room empty. Isabelle called Benz, "If other people call, please tell them we are not receiving callers today, and could you ask Mrs Hopkins to make us fresh tea?"

Benz glanced at Lady Beaumont for confirmation, but the glazed expression and slumped posture suggested that he should take Isabelle's proposition seriously. Isabelle watched her mother, concerned that her well-being was the utmost in her mind. What had the Duke done to cause such a strong reaction in her mother? Isabelle didn't know much about the Duke, and she hazarded a guess that he would be an unknown quantity to the ton, so what did her mother know about the man that caused such an adverse reaction? Isabelle could tell from their brief introduction that he was not a young buck but an older suitor. What would prompt the man to offer to court her when he had never met her before? Was his offer to spite her mother, or was he genuinely interested? When the refreshments arrived, there would be time enough to discover her mother's aversion to the man.

Her optimism was unwarranted as her mother refused to discuss Lord Fagean except to scold her daughter for accepting his invitation. Even with her mother's warnings ringing in her ears, Isabelle admitted that the slightly dangerous air surrounding the Duke intrigued her. A ride in the park would be welcome, and even if it amounted to nothing, the thought of not having to sit through another mind-numbing session with Lord Raven cheered her.

Dinner that night was a strained affair; her mother was seemingly still stunned by the Duke's appearance, so conversation lagged. Lord Beaumont, attempting to foster the discussion, asked the one question that could cause the most controversy.

"Isabelle dear, how goes it with Lord Raven's courtship? Should I expect a visit soon to discuss your marriage prospects?"

Isabelle studied the food on her plate, unsure of her reply. At that moment, Lady Beaumont spoke.

"Lord Raven is sure to make his intentions clear, and when he does, Isabelle will accept his offer. A marriage to the man will keep Isabelle in good standing, and the match's prestige will help me find a suitor in years to come for Rosie and Esme."

Lord Beaumont smiled kindly at his daughter. "That sounds splendid, my dear. Are you excited?"

Isabelle sighed. "No, Father, I'm not excited. The man is a terrible bore, and I'm sure as long as I greet him at the door, I could leave the room, and he would still blather on, unaware that he was alone. He has called ten times without offering to stroll in the park or drive in his carriage, and to be honest, I don't know that he intends to offer for me. He may pay his respects and drink our tea, but he has said nothing that suggests he is ready to offer for me. Mother has failed to reveal that we had another caller who wishes to court me. Lord Fagean, the Duke of Kenmore, is calling for me to ride in the park with him."

Isabelle's father raised his eyebrow.

"Do I know the man?"

Lady Beaumont glared at her daughter.

"The man is a degenerate who has spent years on the continent. He does not have the social standing of Lord Raven, and I do not want Isabelle to associate with the cad."

"Hm, why do you want to go for a ride to the park with this man, Isabelle?"

"Father, I understand that I need to marry and that prospective husbands need to be of good character and social standing, but if I have to live the rest of my life with a man, I would prefer not to be bored to tears. He is the first man who wants to be seen in public with me, and I would enjoy a ride in the park."

"Goodness, Isabelle, any other debutant would happily accept Lord Raven as a husband."

"I'm certain that you are right, but Mother, after you organise a suitable husband for me, you go off on your merry way, and I have to look at the man you approve over breakfast for the rest of my life. You seem to have forgotten that Lord Raven has made no offer or declaration. It wouldn't surprise me if he is stringing me along until someone better presents herself."

"Hazel, Lord Raven hasn't spoken to me about his intentions, so maybe we should let Isabelle meet with the other man. After a few outings, I can talk to both men about their intentions."

Pushing his chair away, he said, " I will retire to the library for my port and leave you two to discuss the suitors."

Isabelle watched her mother in silence after Lord Beaumont left the table. When it appeared that her mother was not intending to speak, Isabelle said,

"Mother, if you tell me why you hate Lord Fagean, I may not find him intriguing, and your concerns would diminish. What did the man do to offend you? Whatever happened was long ago because you said he has been on the continent for years. Unless he has extremely wounded you, isn't it time to forget the slight?"

"I will never forgive that man; all you need to know is that he is unsuitable."

"It's hard to discount a Duke when a lady is looking for a beau. Unless you are willing to tell me what the man did that has you practically swooning with anger, I will accept his invitations until he proves himself unworthy."

"If people see you are gadding about with the likes of him, the news will get back to Lord Raven, and he may withdraw his suit."

"Mother, it seems Lord Raven has had plenty of time to press his suit, and it's telling that he continues to dither. If I were you, I wouldn't build up your hopes; the man does not give me the impression that he is in any hurry to choose a bride. If Lord Raven were looking for a bride and singled me out, you would assume he would do more to press his suit than sit in the sitting room drinking tea and talking. If he is seriously interested in courting me, why have we had no walks in the park? Lord Raven is happy to sit here where no one can see him, and when another caller arrives, he immediately departs. If anyone is a scoundrel, I fear it is Lord Raven, and it might be in my best interests if Father asks him about his intentions before these visits continue. You say my accompanying Lord Fagean will annoy Lord Raven, but who knows? Maybe other suitors have crossed me off their lists, thinking Lord Raven is ready to propose, and if he doesn't come up to scratch, I am at a disadvantage."

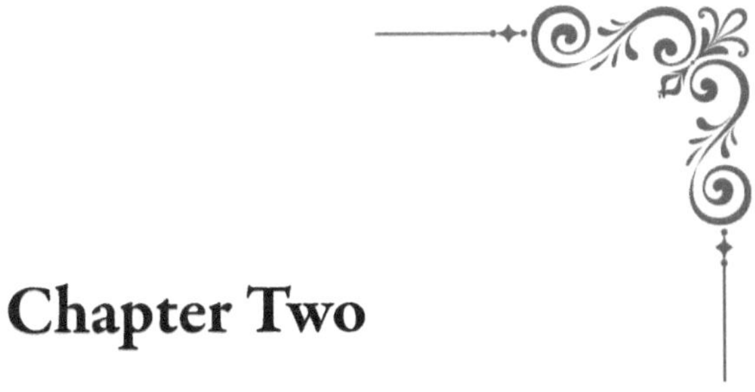

Chapter Two

Isabelle dithered about the appropriate attire for a ride in the park. Bessie made several selections, but Isabelle couldn't decide which outfit looked the best.

"Goodness, Bessie, the choice is so hard. I might not be so anxious about this outing if Lord Raven ever asked me to accompany him to the park. But this is all new to me. Choose an outfit for me, Bessie, and I will trust your judgement."

Dressed in a lemon-coloured floral sundress, Isabelle looked a picture. Bessie tied her matching bonnet securely, and Isabelle walked down the stairs to wait for Lord Fagean.

At the socially accepted time of ten o'clock, Benz announced Lord Fagean's arrival. From their brief interaction yesterday, Isabelle found the man intriguing. Her mother's loathing of the Duke was so far unexplained, and she hoped the man might satisfy her curiosity. Isabelle's father would have the man investigated if this carriage ride became more than a dalliance, and if he was all that her mother claimed, their rides might be short-lived.

It surprised Isabelle when the man arrived in a curricle, not the carriage he had initially invited her to share. Still, the smaller open vehicle meant that a chaperone was unnecessary. A chaperone would monitor the interaction between the occupants, encouraging them to discuss new ribbons and bonnets. How could one get to know someone else when the conversation was so mindless? Whenever Isabelle had initiated a discussion with Lord Raven, he would pat her on the hand, smile benevolently, and continue with his dialogue. So, this opportunity to get to know Lord Fagean without the constraints of a chaperone was one that Isabelle relished.

Once Lord Fagean assisted Isabelle in seating herself, he jogged to his side of the carriage and sprang aboard. Isabelle didn't begin talking until Lord Fagean had manoeuvred his horses onto the road. It was the perfect day for an open carriage, and with her bonnet tied firmly in place, Isabelle enjoyed the breeze on her face and the sun's warmth. With her face tilted towards the sun, Isabelle paid little heed to the Duke, so when he spoke, he jolted her out of her daze.

"Well, my lady, tell me about yourself."

Isabelle smiled. "What, my Lord, you don't want to hear about the new ribbons I purchased yesterday or my lovely new bonnet? I'm shocked."

Lord Fagean turned his attention from the road to glance at Isabelle.

"With a mother like yours, I assumed you would be a young lady lacking fire and enthusiasm, but it appears I am wrong."

"I'll ignore the slight against my mother because the animosity comes from you both, and I don't want to get in the middle of a skirmish between you two. Why did you ask me to ride with you if you thought I'd be dull? Is this ride a form of revenge for some wrong done to my mother? I asked her what the problem was with you, but she kept saying you were debauched and I should decline your invitation."

" I invited you to ride with me because I need a wife, and my friend Gareth Smyth said you conducted yourself like a lady; he felt confident that Johnathon Raven was stringing you along. He has sisters and said if Raven treated them in the same cavalier manner he treats you, he'd take the fellow out and beat him."

"Someone else thinks Lord Raven isn't committed to this courtship. I said the same to my mother, but she believed he would come up to scratch. But you have to wonder about a man who is supposed to be courting me, but never accompanies me anywhere. He sits in the parlour drinking tea, and we never venture past the front door. You say you are not driving in the park with me as revenge, and I'm glad you aren't, but will you tell me what the antagonism is between you and my mother?"

Lord Fagean watched the animated expression of his companion, and an uneasy silence settled between them. He felt a momentary stab of guilt, questioning if this was the best strategy, but pushed it aside when the face of his tormentor flashed in his brain. He knew he could tell a lie with conviction, but realised that he felt terrible about lying to this naive miss.

"Your mother and I knew one another when I was eighteen and she was twenty-two. There was an incident, and she's blamed me ever since, although she was at fault, not me. I might tell you the story one day, but not today. I want to talk to a young lady with more conversation skills than most airheaded debutants I've met."

Zavier Fagean steered the curricle around the park's winding footpaths as the conversation flowed. Oblivious to the scrutiny of the other inhabitants of carriages and other conveyances, Isabelle related the little there was to say about her life, but listened with rapt attention as Zavier described some of the sights he saw while travelling the globe. The

time seemed to fly by, and when Zavier stopped at her front door, Isabelle felt sad. Today, she had enjoyed herself more than with any other man, and she wondered if this was a solitary excursion. Zavier assisted Isabelle in leaving the vehicle and escorted her to the door. With a bow, he stepped away from her and then searched her face before he said,

"May I call on you tomorrow?"

Isabelle smiled, the pleasure at being invited to spend time with Lord Fagean evident on her face.

"Thank you for the excursion to the park today, Your Grace. Yes, you may call tomorrow."

Benz opened the door, and Zavier watched Isabelle go, feeling dread in his stomach. This dalliance with the daughter of the woman he hated was supposed to be sweet revenge, and growing to admire the chit was not part of his plan. He had hated the Beaumont woman with a vengeance since his father had exiled him at the age of eighteen, and he needed to stay focused on his goal. Zavier flicked a coin at the boy holding the horse's reins and vaulted into the curricle.

When he returned home, Zavier reviewed his plan; he wanted to spend as much time as possible alone with Isabelle to ensure she was an ardent admirer of him. Once he had Isabelle expecting more, he would venture to some of the unending social activities the ton's members organised and make their connection public. Standing the girl up in a crowd would cause her some distress, but it should make her mother furious. For once, the woman who was the bane of his existence could suffer humiliation and regret.

When he discussed his plan with his friend, Gareth, the amusement and admiration he expected weren't forthcoming. Gareth pointed out that Zavier's argument was with Lady Beaumont, and disgracing the innocent daughter of his adversary was not the right way to exact revenge on the woman. Even though his friend Garreth seemed shocked at Zavier's proposed treatment of the Beaumont chit, his disapproval wouldn't stop Zavier's course. He had waited too long to avenge the injustice caused by the woman's claims, and now that he had the girl in his sights, nothing could stop him.

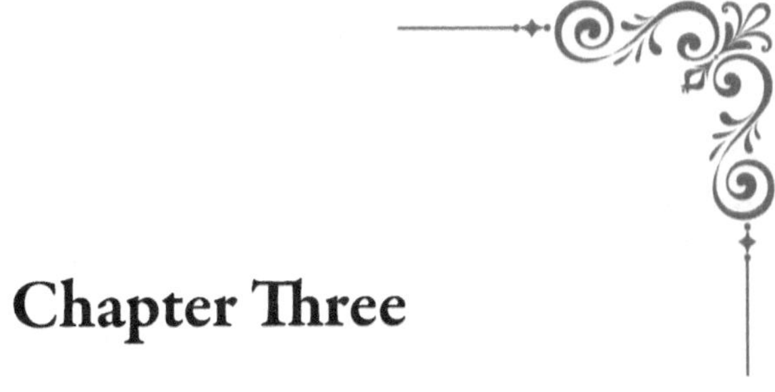

Chapter Three

Isabelle's drive with Lord Fagean left her giddy with excitement. Her mother's warning of dire consequences went unheard as Isabelle joined Zavier on walks in the park, browsing the shops, and even visiting the museum, where he showed her the culture of some of the countries he travelled through. His planned excursions were exciting, but his presence made the outings even more thrilling. Lord Fagean was so handsome, and when he looked at her, Isabelle's heart raced. She wanted to share her excitement and concerns with someone, but her sisters were younger than her, and Isabelle had no friends among the debutantes currently hunting for husbands. An idea had circulated in Isabelle's mind for a while, and she gathered her courage on her next excursion with Lord Fagean and asked for an introduction to his friend's sisters. Her request shocked him, and while blushing furiously, Isabelle scrambled to explain.

"I thought from our first conversation that Lord Smyth's sisters were my age, and I have no friends among the debutants this season. Even with my sisters, a girl wants friends, and I thought you might be open to introducing them to me. I'm sorry; it was presumptuous of me even to ask."

Zavier's silence caused Isabelle anguish; had she ruined her chances with the Duke because she asked the impossible? Zavier tossed the idea around in his brain, and the one critical thought that plagued him was that if Isabelle was friends with the Smyth sisters, the repercussions of his revenge might affect them. Isabelle's request was as troubling as it was unexpected. Should he tell her that Garreth's sisters were too young to be considered friends? The problem with lying about their ages was that if she came in contact with them at an event, it would raise questions about his honesty with Isabelle.

"Why don't I ask Garreth and let him make the decision? I can't see the harm in asking."

Isabelle sighed with relief. "Thank you, my Lord. I'd appreciate that."

Isabelle and Zavier were quiet after his answer, and Isabelle felt that he would end their time together, and it would be her fault. To her surprise, Zavier said, "Let's get going; we should have time to visit the fountain in the main square. You can toss a penny into the water and make a wish."

Isabelle smiled. "You always think of unusual things to do. Why do other men want to sit inside, drink tea, and discuss the weather? And many men talk endlessly about their horses or wealth and ignore their partner's conversation?"

Zavier grinned. "That, my dear, is because mothers teach their daughters that men don't like intelligent women."

"And is that true? Do men like dumb women?"

Zavier let out a chortle. "Only you would ask that, and yes, some men prefer dumb women. Smart ladies tend to argue more, and if they are too dumb to work out their husbands' transgressions, the men's lives are easier."

"I suppose I understand what you're saying, but the thought of living with a man who never wants to discuss anything more than how tender the meat is would drive me to distraction."

Standing next to the fountain, Isabelle considered Zavier's opinion of women. Was she too outspoken, and did the men who steered away from her consider her too intelligent? How did you find a suitor who liked wise women? Zavier interrupted her thoughts when he held out a penny for her. For now, Isabelle was happy being escorted around town by Zavier, but he hadn't been to any of the social events she frequented.

"Why don't you make a wish? I'm unsure if they come true, but it doesn't hurt to have a go."

Isabelle took the penny and closed her eyes. As Zavier watched her, he guessed what she wished but did not comment. When Isabelle tossed her penny into the water, she blushed as she saw Zavier watching her. Isabelle hated being so transparent, but she had enjoyed her outings with Zavier and hoped he would speak to her father about seriously considering her as a partner. The couple strolled around the park surrounding the fountain, and then something extraordinary happened: Zavier asked if she was attending the Birchmoore's ball and if she would save a dance for him.

As Isabelle prepared for the ball that afternoon, her mother entered the room. Isabelle tensed, expecting her mother to complain about the number of outings she shared with Zavier. No matter what her mother said about him being a cad and a liar, Isabelle hadn't caught him in an untruth, and he hadn't tried to convince her to kiss him or hold his hand. If her mother told her of the problem between her and Lord Fagean, she might see her mother's point of view, but from where she was standing, Zavier seemed to be the perfect man for her.

"Isabelle, you need to make more effort at the ball tonight. We are halfway through the season, and you don't have any men interested in you. If you hadn't spent so much time with that damned Fagean, I'm confident Lord Raven would have offered for you. You must forget Fagean and find a man serious about finding a wife."

"Mother Lord Raven had no intention of offering for me, and I said that when he spent endless hours drinking tea and telling us how wonderful he is. He was waiting for an American heiress to come on the scene, and his defection was swift once that debutant from Dickerson appeared. I can smile and be polite, but I can't make gentlemen take notice of me. The only man who seems interested is Lord Fagean, and even if he is not looking for a bride, I enjoy his company. He is exciting and considerate; we have not discussed the weather or my new bonnets, and most other gentlemen seem to think women are too stupid to discuss anything else."

"Mark my words, Isabelle; he is dallying with you to keep himself amused while he searches for the right woman. He is with you to pay me back and thinks he can get revenge by escorting you. The more time you spend with that cad, the more he can hurt and humiliate you. You must find a good man and set your sights on him."

Isabelle nodded, knowing that her mother would continue to harass her until she conceded. Her surrender to her mother's wishes in the bedroom didn't mean that she intended to ignore Lord Fagean when he arrived tonight. Her mother's constant warnings against Lord Fagean were tiresome, and her refusal to give reasons caused Isabelle to disregard any caution she might have otherwise exercised.

Chapter Four

Isabelle danced with the men who had written their names on her dance card at the beginning of the evening, but when her card was almost complete, she declined the last few offers. Keeping her mother from realising that her card was not full took some manoeuvring, but she would not miss out on dancing when Lord Fagean came. As the evening wore on, she realised that she hadn't asked what time he intended to make an appearance, and Isabelle feared that she had made a mistake by not filling her card on the assumption that he would be here and ask her to dance.

When the conductor called the next dance, Lady Beaumont badgered Isabelle to make eye contact with her next partner, only to realise that Isabelle didn't have a partner. Before she could berate Isabelle for her foolishness, Lord Fagean was at her side. He bowed over her hand, and Isabelle grinned and hooked her arm through his as he moved them to the dance floor. The two dances Isabel left vacant were waltzes, so not only could she feel the strength of his body against hers, but, unlike the reels where they separated, she could talk to him.

"I was beginning to think that you were not coming. My mother said I could not dance with you, and it took some fiddling to keep her unaware of the two dances I left vacant."

Zavier looked at her upturned face; she was slightly flushed, with either the exertions of dancing or his proximity. A pang of guilt hit him; should he abandon his revenge and court the girl seriously? A sudden thought of the woman who had ruined him, as his mother-in-law wiped his fanciful ideas from his mind.

"I didn't want to arrive too soon in case your mother packed you into the coach and drove home."

As Zavier spun her around, Isabelle decided that this rush of emotion was what she missed with the other men who danced with her. How could she settle for a comfortable man when she could have an exciting and romantic courtship with this man? Much to her regret, the dance ended, and Zavier moved a respectable distance from Isabelle.

"My Lord, will you have supper with me?"

"Do you think your mother would approve?"

"No, but she won't make a fuss publicly; she will wait till we get home to tell me off."

Zavier grinned. "My brave little debutant! Yes, I will have supper with you and hope that the private punishment for you is not too great."

Zavier was a considerate partner, selecting food for Isabel and delivering their drinks. Isabel caught the glance of other ladies who watched as Zavier chatted to her, and a feeling of unease filled her. Why was a handsome, mature man like Lord Fagean squiring her around town? From the looks on the ladies' faces, he could have them as his companions instead of escorting a nobody. Isabelle tried to push her unwanted thoughts away and enjoy what she had for the time being. As supper concluded, Isabelle sighed.

"Will you ask other ladies to dance while you wait for the next waltz?"

Lord Fagean grinned. "Jealous, are you? I came to dance with you, sweetheart, not other women."

"Oh, no. I just.."

Isabelle could feel her face flush, and she ducked her head. Lord Fagean made her feel like a twelve-year-old; had he expected an answer to his question? Her heart raced when he called her sweetheart, but she managed to subdue her reaction to him.

"I saved another dance for you if you want to stay longer. I filled my card but left the waltzes vacant because I don't want strangers to hold me close."

"Then why did you allow me to waltz with you?"

Isabelle blushed and averted her face. Zavier held her chin between his thumb and forefinger and turned her head towards him.

"Isabelle, look at me. Why did you let me hold you close?"

"Because I like you more than any of the other men."

Zavier grinned. "Good. Make sure you save all your waltzes for me."

When Isabelle's next partner arrived, she had no alternative but to move onto the dance floor with him. The dances seemed to take an eternity, and Isabelle was eager to finish with these partners and once again be held in the strong arms of Lord Fagean. After the dance, before the waltz concluded, Isabelle looked around for Zavier. Before she located him, a man presented himself to her and held out his hand. Isabelle stepped back as she scanned the room. When she saw Zavier leaning against the wall, she frowned at him. Why had he not moved towards her to claim the last dance?

"Lady Isabelle, I believe this is my dance."

Isabelle looked at the stranger and said, "I fear there is some confusion here. I already have a partner for this dance."

Beckoning at Zavier, Isabelle glared at him. Could the man not come and claim his dance? As he strolled towards her, the other man gripped her hand and placed it on his arm.

Isabelle wrenched her arm away from the man and stomped her foot.

"I have explained that I have a partner for this dance, and as you didn't fill out my card, I am confused about why you think I would dance with you. I don't know your name, and it is improper of you to approach me without an introduction."

Isabelle reached for Zavier with a relieved sigh as he stood close to her.

"I believe, my dear, that your mother may have orchestrated this problem."

He tucked her hand in his arm and looked over his shoulder at the glaring man.

"Sorry, old man. If you want to dance with Isabelle, you will have to wait until next time, and you should fill out her card like the rest of her partners."

The man stormed off as the orchestra played the first line of the waltz, and Zavier took the proper stance, although he held her closer than was considered respectable. Isabelle didn't care that the old biddies glared and whispered. She had attended social events where partners took liberties, even though the debutants attempted to maintain a respectable distance from them. Instead of supporting the girls, the matrons labelled them as fast and never rebuked the men. When the waltz finished, Lord Fagean bowed over Isabelle's hand and said, "I had better leave before your mother embarrasses us all. Can I call tomorrow?"

"Yes, please."

Isabelle watched him as he left. How had she been lucky enough to have this handsome, suitable man court her? Before he exited, he turned to see her watching him, and he smiled and winked before disappearing.

The carriage ride home was silent, and her mother glared whenever their eyes met. Isabelle did not care that her mother was giving her the silent treatment; it meant she could relive the dances with Lord Fagean without interruption. Unfortunately, the silent treatment ended as they entered the front door. Lady Beaumont snapped at Benz and ordered Isabelle to go into the parlour. Lord Beaumont meandered past just as the maid placed the refreshments on the low table. He looked at Isabelle's glowing face and the angry expression on his wife's face and frowned. How could his daughter look blissfully happy and his wife livid?

"Did you have a nice time, ladies?"

Isabell grinned. "I had a lovely time; thank you, Father."

Lady Beaumont glared at her daughter before she commenced her tirade.

"Isabelle saved both waltzes for that bounder Fagean and turned down an invitation to dance with Lord Childers, the Earl of Winchester. Fagean is toying with Isabelle, and she should find a suitable beau, but she is besotted with the man, and he will walk away from her rather than commit."

"Why do you think he will desert her after courting her? He seems attentive and considerate; what purpose is there in shaming Isabelle?"

"Nobody listens to me. I knew the man many years ago, and he is a good-for-nothing scoundrel who has lived a debauched life on the continent for years. Any interest he has in Isabelle is fleeting, and an association with the man will ruin her."

Clifford Beaumont shook his head.

"My dear, my investigator probed into his background, and he seems to be a worthwhile candidate. He returned from the continent six months ago because his father was dying. The new Lord Raegan took over the estate when the old Duke died. The estate was in poor condition when he inherited it, as his father had been ill for a long time, and the steward was not fulfilling his duties. The investigator heard about a scandal concerning the young heir, and as a result, his father sent him to the continent. My man couldn't get any more details, but whatever the trouble was when the Duke was young, he appears to have sorted himself out."

Lady Beaumont intervened. "The scandal may resurface, and if he and Isabelle are together, the shame will spill over to her."

Isabelle interrupted the dissection of Lord Fagean's character.

"Mother, you keep warning me away from Lord Fagean, and unless you give me a reason to avoid the man, I will continue to keep him company. He treats me well, takes no liberties and thinks of interesting excursions. I hope your assessment that he is only dallying with me is inaccurate, and he comes up to the mark."

"Well, I should meet this man and ask what his intentions are towards you, Isabelle. There's no use pining after a man unless he shows interest in you becoming his wife."

"Thank you, Father. A meeting with the Duke is a sterling idea."

Chapter Five

Isabelle trusted her father to follow up on the interview with Lord Fagean, but today would not be the day the discussion occurred, as her father was away on business. After her father's pronouncement, Isabelle worried he would ask Lord Fagean about his intentions toward his daughter. What if the Duke told her father that he didn't intend to take the courtship further, and her father called a halt to their excursions? Isabelle's thoughts distracted her, and she wasn't ready when Lord Fagean called for her. She sent her maid to ask Benz to apologise and ask the Duke to wait in the parlour. After a quick change and a wash, Isabelle hurried towards the parlour. Before she could tell Benz to open the door, he shook his head and touched her arm. The unexpected touch shocked Isabelle, and she swung to look at the butler. Benz quietly spoke as he removed his hand.

"I beg your pardon, Miss Isabelle, but as your mother and the Duke are arguing, it is best to wait until the shouting dies down, and I can announce you."

Isabelle turned to face the door, and the sound of the altercation became more evident as the combatants moved closer to the partially open door.

"You are only courting my daughter to spite me; leave her alone; she has nothing to do with our differences."

Lord Fagean's laugh was like nothing Isabelle had heard from him; he sounded slightly maniacal and not the gentleman she knew. When he spoke, the hard edge to his voice concerned her; what on earth was happening?

" Of course, I am only courting your daughter to avenge the hell you put me through. I would have thought a brash, pushy woman like you would have a bold, nosy daughter. Imagine my surprise when I met a sweet, naive young woman; convincing her of my honourable intentions was easy. My revenge will be complete when I ruin her."

In the hallway, Isabelle and Benz stood transfixed as the ugly duplicity of the Duke's plan became apparent. Benz came to his senses first and moved Isabelle away from the door. Her shocked, pale face stood out starkly in the dim hallway, and Benz knew that, regardless of propriety, he had to move her to her bedroom. With his hand resting on her arm, he said,

"My Lady, you need to retire to the bedroom. I will send Bessie to help you, and I will send the bounder on his way."

Isabelle nodded and allowed Benz to steer her to her room. As the butler retreated, the ugly, hateful words Lord Fagean spewed out rang in her ears. The man was a cad, and had she not heard that argument, she would have mindlessly followed his lead until he ruined her. Her mother was right. When her maid entered the room, the tears began to flow, and Isabelle allowed the girl to remove her dress and bundle her into bed.

The argument in the parlour seemed to have dissipated, and Benz knocked on the door. He pushed the door open, and the two enemies stood facing each other when he entered. Benz cleared his throat and said, "My Lord, I regret to inform you that Lady Isabelle will not be accompanying you today or any day in the future. She has clarified that she does not wish to see you again."

Lord Fagean groaned as he realised he had ruined his chances with Isabelle because of a lack of self-control when the Beaumont woman accosted him. He stalked towards the entry and grabbed his hat as Benz opened the door with a flourish. No doubt, the butler had heard what he said, so there was no hope of getting around the man in the future. If Isabelle had listened to the hateful things he said, there would be no way to retract or apologise for his comments.

That night, after Fagean had devoured half of the new bottle of whisky, his butler announced the arrival of his friend Gareth. Zavier waved a glass at his friend.

"Join me; I'm drowning my sorrows."

Gareth collected a glass from the sideboard and took the proffered bottle from Zavier.

"What tragedy has befallen you that requires you to drown your sorrows?"

"When I arrived to collect Isabelle, she was running late. The butler deposited me in the parlour to wait for her, and that horrid Beaumont woman entered the room. We got into a slanging match, and I revealed that I was courting Isabelle as revenge for what the woman did to me, and I fear Isabelle and the butler overheard. The butler entered the room a few minutes later and said that Isabelle would not be accompanying me today or any day in the future. She does not wish to see me again."

Gareth let out a whistle. "You broke the chit's heart without even trying. Leave her alone, Zavier; she is not responsible for what happened between her mother and you. Her mother is such a cold-hearted baggage that ruining her daughter will not devastate her, and she will find some rich man to marry Isabelle regardless of what you do."

"Maybe you're right. I felt uncomfortable lying to the girl. She is so innocent and unsuspecting that deceiving her is easy. I hope her mother doesn't marry her to a rich old man; if Lady Beaumont weren't her mother, I would offer for her because she is unlike the insipid debutantes who spend their lives discussing the weather and their newest bonnet."

"You entered society to snag a wife and wreak havoc on Lady Beaumont. Now, your plans for revenge are scuttled; what will you do about snagging a suitable woman?"

"I hear tell there is an American heiress who is looking for a title. I might make myself known to her and see where it leads. If she is looking for a title, my finances are up to scratch, so she'll know I'm not after her money."

"Whatever your plans were for Isabelle, please leave her alone. Please don't hurt her any further. Your revenge will force her to marry some old man who wants a broodmare, and her life will be full of humiliation and heartache. I never liked your scheme, and thankfully, she heard the argument and extricated herself from the situation before you could do her irreparable damage. Put it behind you; you can do nothing to recover those lost years."

Once Gareth departed, Zavier reviewed his behaviour over the last six weeks. Was Gareth correct in his assessment of the woman's feelings for Isabelle? Would her mother sell her to one of the debauched aristocrats who wanted an heir but didn't want a wife? He felt a tinge of regret when he thought of the grief he had caused Isabelle, but with his arch nemesis beyond his powers of revenge, he decided to cause the woman pain through association. He could not do anything now, so it would be best to put the whole mess behind him and move forward to make his acquaintance with the American heiress.

Chapter Six

The days since Lord Fagean revealed his true purpose in courting Isabelle as revenge were a torment. Her mother had not given Isabelle a moment to grieve the dissolution of her relationship with the one man who interested her. Isabelle had no desire to attend social events, but her mother was not to be thwarted. The purpose of being in society for a debutant was to find a husband, and Hazel Beaumont intended to see her daughter wed.

Her mother chivvied Isabelle along as they descended from the coach. Despite Isabelle's protestations, her mother would not be swayed, and because of Lord Fagaen's plot, Isabelle left her run a bit late. Some unattached men met Lady Beaumont's criteria, so she hustled Isabelle from group to group, hoping for commitments by writing their names on the dance card. Once Lady Beaumont had Isabelle's card filled, she felt pleased. Lord Fagean would not ruin Isabelle's chances, although her reputation had taken a hit due to her close association with the man. Even though some men who committed to dance with Isabelle were borderline acceptable, Lady Beaumont thought she could steer her daughter toward an appropriate marriage.

As Isabelle suffered one after another dance partner she had no interest in, she recalled the last ball she had attended. Fool that she was, she had saved the waltzes for Lord Fagean and was even fool enough to tell him why she wanted to dance the waltzes with him. How long would the cad have continued his deception? What scandal had occurred involving her mother and Lord Fagean that had affected their lives so much? If Isabelle had to pay the price for a humiliating incident involving her mother and Lord Fagean, shouldn't she have the right to know the details?

Isabelle's focus returned swiftly as her dance partner pulled her in closer. She could feel the protruding belly that seemed a feature of all the men who danced with her tonight, and his sweaty palm rested too low on her waist. As she wriggled to make room between them, her partner grinned.

"No use pretending you're still a maiden after the time you spent with that Lothario Fagean. He wouldn't keep you around for long if you weren't warming his bed. I think I'm going to enjoy courting you."

Isabelle staggered, and the man glared at her. Did all the men her mother coerced into signing her card believe she was no longer a maiden? Her response was automatic when the man's hand wandered to her backside. Lifting her knee quickly, she jammed it into his crotch and walked away from the man writhing on the ground. Striding past her horrified mother, Isabelle headed for the retiring room. She wasn't interested in saving her reputation if it meant being insulted and pawed over by filthy old men.

When the door slammed open, Isabelle knew it was her mother even though she was facing away from the room's entrance. Her patience had frayed, and the tears that welled were only minutes away from spilling down her cheeks.

"What on earth do you think you are doing? I shudder to think what you did to have that man writhing around on the ground, but I doubt that any of the men who put their name on your card will bother to arrive for their dance."

"If they are all dirty old men who assume I am no longer a maiden and will warm their beds if they say they are courting me, I don't want to dance with them. I don't wish to dance with them if they can take liberties on the dance floor. They would be better off forgetting a respectable ball and heading to one of the bawdy houses. Where did you meet these degenerates who had signed my card? Are you so cowed by society that you would willingly sell me to one of those awful men?"

"Those men you describe as awful are all heirs of the realm and far better men than that Casanova Fagean who fascinated you. At least these men are looking for wives."

"Well, the last one wasn't; he was looking for a woman to warm his bed. And Lord Fagean never pawed me or made inappropriate comments."

Lady Beaumont sighed. "Wash your face and come back into the ballroom. We'll see if we can rescue your evening."

Isabelle watched her mother depart, despair lodged in her heart. How could she pretend to be interested in other men when that cad Fagean had captured her heart? Isabelle did a repair job on her crushed skirt and loose hair and walked towards the ballroom. A quick scan revealed the absence of the man she had left writhing on the floor; she felt relieved that he wouldn't be available for the second dance he had signed for.

Isabelle stood beside her mother, a fake smile on her face, wondering if the men who had signed her card would present themselves for their dance. While she waited, she glanced around the room. The red-headed American heiress seemed to be the centre of attention as men vied for her acceptance. Isabelle's heart stuttered when she realised that the man leading the woman onto the dance floor was Lord Fagean. As he walked past her, he smiled and winked at her. Isabelle's fake smile slid off her face as a stab of pain lodged in her heart. How could he be so cruel as to flaunt another woman in her face after destroying her hopes and dreams? Watching the man who captured her interest and her heart twirl another lady around the dance floor was too painful.

"Mother, my next partner has not arrived, and I require a break."

Her mother sighed, aware of the reason for Isabelle's downturned mouth.

"Go, but don't venture too far into the house; perhaps the library will give you the peace you need?"

Once Lady Beaumont approved Isabelle's suggestion, she wasted no time leaving the ballroom. Her mother had recommended the library, and Isabelle thought any room would do; she needed time away from watching Lord Fagean with his new conquest. Her heart ached as Isabelle realised that not only had Lord Fagean moved on, but he was searching for a bride, and the American heiress had everything he wanted in a woman. She was beautiful, outgoing and rich. What more could a man want? The woman had made it clear to her bevy of admirers that she was looking for a title, and what better title could she hope for than a duke?

As Isabelle wandered from row to row, she heard the door click, and the music volume increased as someone entered the room. Isabelle's night could not get any worse unless this were her mother coming to check on her.

"Isabelle, we need to talk."

The deep male voice made Isabelle's heart clench, and she swung around to find Lord Fagean standing there.

"What have we to discuss, my Lord? I am too young, too innocent and too naive for your tastes. You clarified your opinion the other day when you confessed that you were courting me because of your hatred of my mother. Return to the American woman; she has the attributes you want."

Zavier ran his hand through his previously coiffed hair. Tonight, he looked uncomfortable for the first time since she met Lord Fagean. But she was immune to his discomfort.

"Isabelle, I didn't think my plan for revenge would work, and while I intended to ruin you to devastate your mother, it seems to have backfired because she doesn't look in the least upset."

"Is that supposed to be an apology? Is that supposed to make me feel all warm and fuzzy when another debauched old man dances with me? Will that calm my mind while my mother tries to badger me into marrying one of the highly regarded aristocrats? Some men dancing with me believe you wouldn't have kept me around so long unless I was warming your bed and aim to court me to have the same privileges. Thanks to you, I have been insulted and pawed. Get out of here before you compromise me any further."

Zavier cringed at the description of Isabelle's dancing partners tonight. He had wanted this, determined to devastate Lady Beaumont. Still, from the men who had danced with Isabelle tonight, she had doubled down on getting her daughter married off, and she wasn't particular about who Isabelle's prospective husband might be. He should leave; nothing he said could repair the damage he had done to this innocent, naive girl.

No sooner had the words left her mouth than the voices of people walking along the hallway registered. Isabelle looked frantically around. Could they hide amongst the shelves? As she considered her options, the door flew open. A gaggle of people stood gaping at the entrance, and Isabelle felt a sinking feeling in her stomach. This man, who had ruined her, had now compromised her, and she knew he would not step up and marry her. Isabelle's vision dimmed as she stood still in the room while the gossipers and curiosity seekers gawked at her.

Zavier stalked to the door.

"There is nothing to see here. We are both fully clothed, and there has been no impropriety. Lady Isabelle and I discussed a problem, and you will not shame me into marrying the chit. The bitch has done this to me once before, but this time I will not disappear overseas. Get out of the way."

Isabelle sank onto the settee behind her and put her face in her hands. She didn't remember leaving the library; the journey home was a blur of sensations and felt unreal. The unexpected sympathy from her mother stunned Isabelle. Still, she knew that come the morning, her mother would have a plan to marry Isabelle off to reduce the scandal that might affect her sister's chances in the next few years. Considering the men her mother had chosen as likely suitors tonight, she cringed at how her future would look. How could falling in love with a man end so badly? If marrying one of the aristocrats she had met that night were her only option, Isabelle decided she would rather retire to a cottage in the country and live alone.

Chapter Seven

Lord Beaumont fumed as his wife divulged the events of the evening. It shocked him to think that the Duke had wanted to ruin Isabelle, and yet he still managed to achieve his goal after she cut ties with him. He noticed the distress on his wife's face and could only imagine how Isabelle felt. What had possessed her to meet the man in private? Most of his questions would have to wait until tomorrow, but one thing his wife made clear was that Lord Fagean had been adamant about refusing to marry Isabelle. There would be no marriage document and no last-minute reprieve for Isabelle.

"What options are open to us, Hazel? I hate to think of Isabelle alone for the rest of her life."

"After what went down tonight, I doubt we have many options. Perhaps we should look for a husband on the continent or send her to the Americas to find a suitable partner. Before the debacle, I introduced Isabelle to the older men in the room, and most of them signed her card and showed interest. Isabel showed no interest in any of them, and Simon Montague landed on the floor, writhing in pain after Isabel danced with him, and she complained that he groped and insulted her."

Lord Beaumont laughed. "That's my girl."

Hazel Beaumont huffed. "I'm not sure what she did to him, although I can hazard a guess. When other men realise what happened to Simon Montague, they will give Isabelle a wide berth. If I can't get her married off, so the scandal dies, Esme and Rose may be plagued by the rumours when it comes to their turn."

Clifford Beaumont scoffed. "For goodness' sake, Esme is only twelve, and Rose is ten. A thousand other scandals will have come and gone before they make their debuts. We will talk to Isabelle in the morning and ask why she spoke to the man privately. Then we can devise a strategy to overcome the problem you and Lord Fagean caused."

Lady Beaumont let out a shriek of anger.

"I didn't cause any problem. I told Isabelle continuously that the man was depraved and she should steer clear. You did nothing to dissuade her, even after I told you what type of man he was, so how this is my fault eludes me."

Clifford Beaumont observed his wife. It was evident to him that she was hiding something which she had no intention of revealing."If you had told Isabelle what the man did to you, she might not have ignored your warning. I heard her ask at least twice for you to explain, and you refused to say anything except that he was a scoundrel. As it turns out, you were right, but your comment would have had more impact if we knew the details of the incident."

"I have no intention of reliving that dark time in my life; it should have been enough for her to believe me regardless of long, involved descriptions."

"I suppose we must wait until tomorrow to discover what happened."

Isabelle hid in her bedroom the following day, reluctant to face her mother's wrath. Lady Beaumont refused to allow her to eat in her room, so hunger was the driving force that caused Isabelle to leave her room. When she presented herself in the breakfast room, her mother surveyed her messy hair, wrinkled dress and the black smudges under her red, swollen eyes.

"Good grief, Isabelle, should I fire your lady's maid? Turning you out looking like a homeless person is not why we pay the girl. Call her in here; I will give her her marching orders."

"Please, Mother, my appearance is not due to Bethie's inability; I didn't feel like getting dressed to the nines for breakfast."

"Dressing well is not considered dressing to the nines, and arriving late insults those who have already arrived. Call the girl to tidy you up, and then come for breakfast."

When Isabell returned, the maid had confined her hair in a neat bun; her dress was a fresh green sundress, and her eyes were a bit clearer. To the uninformed observer, the family appeared relaxed and at ease, but the underlying tension was evident in the eyes of Isabelle and her parents. The conversation over breakfast was general, and Esme and Rose discussed taking a ride after their governess finished their lessons. After the meal, Lady Beaumont shooed the two girls off to meet their governess, and she and Lord Beaumont suggested they retire to the library.

Clifford Beaumont said, "Sit, Isabelle and tell me what happened last night. We can't move forward until we deal with the outstanding issues."

As Isabelle related the incidents of the night before, her father frowned.

"Lord Montague said that the only reason Lord Fagean would keep me around for so long was that I was warming his bed. He said he was interested in that kind of courtship, then placed his hand on my derriere. I kneed him in the groin and walked off the dance floor while he writhed around like a beached whale."

Lady Beaumont looked slightly green.

"Goodness gracious, I can't believe he behaved like that. I would never have asked him to dance with you if I had known. That's why you said you needed a timeout."

"Partly. As I walked back to you, Lord Fagean and the American heiress walked to the dance floor, and he grinned at me and winked. I felt sick and humiliated. I had to leave for a while, but it never occurred to me that he would follow."

"So you're saying he followed you into the room?"

"Yes."

"So he reached his goal of ruining you."

"Yes, but in his defence, I don't think he intended anyone to see us. He apologised for the distress he caused me, but justified it by saying he wanted to pay my mother back for the havoc she caused in his life. I don't know where those people came from, but he lost his cool and shouted when they arrived. But one thing is clear: he intends to court the American heiress, and she wants a title so they will make a match of it."

Lady Beaumont tapped the table with her fingernails.

"So now we have to devise a strategy to minimise this incident's effect on you and your sisters. We could go to the continent and find a husband, but that will take quite some time to arrange. Clifford, do you know any businessmen or merchants who would suit Isabelle?"

Lord Beaumont looked pensive. "The younger men are looking to establish their business, but a few older decent chaps might be ready to settle. Let me think about this, and I'll send some letters."

"Please don't set me up with anyone. I've been considering my options, and I'd like to move to the convent in Bakersville. No scandal will follow me, which will affect my sister's chances of making a good match. No decent man would consider taking me for a wife, so the convent is a good solution."

Lord Beaumont looked horrified, but Lady Beaumont could see sense in the suggestion. If Isabelle were to move to the convent, whether or not she became a nun, her absence from the house would give them all a reprieve. And goodness knows, Isabelle was a liability they couldn't afford with two more girls to introduce into society.

"I think that would be an admirable solution. We need to make enquiries, and with any luck, we can wrap things up in a week or two."

Lord Beaumont turned his face toward Isabelle, his grief showing clearly

"Dear God, do we have to take such drastic measures? Your life will be full of scrubbing, weeding, and praying. Your bed will be a pallet on the floor, and the food will be what you can grow and nothing else. Can't we think of another solution?"

"My lord, Isabelle's solution is the best we can do."

"I know my solution isn't ideal, but I need to be with people who won't give me the cut direct or snigger and gossip behind their fans. Life at the convent will be different from anything I'm used to, but the quiet and the acceptance by the nuns will give me some respite. I don't have the devotion to become a nun, but retiring from the public will allow Esme and Rose to find decent husbands."

Lady Beaumont nodded. "I think it is an excellent idea."

When Isabelle looked at her father, she could see the distress her suggestion caused him. Still, she knew her mother's eagerness to rid herself of her troublesome daughter would overshadow her father's reluctance.

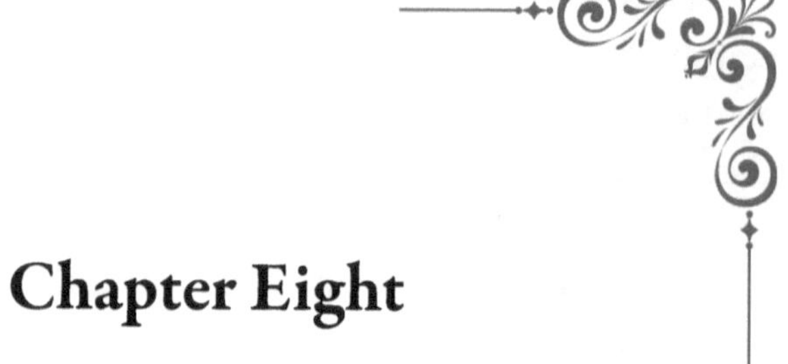

Chapter Eight

Isabelle sat in the parlour, her needlework resting on her knee. How could her season have turned out so disastrously? If her mother had told her what Lord Fagean had done, she might have listened to her mother's assassination of the man's character, but apart from curses and insults about Lord Fagean, her mother refused to tell of the Lord's misdeeds. Isabelle considered her mother's reluctance to share her information regarding Lord Fagean. It suddenly occurred to her that if Lord Fagean had wronged her mother, why was he angry that he was caught and exiled by his father, or was it something else? Isabelle sighed. Would she ever make sense of this disaster that had befallen her?

A tap on the door interrupted her musings, and when she lifted her weary eyes to Benz, he said, "Miss Isabelle, there is a man to see you. I told him you weren't receiving visitors, but he asked me to tell you that Lord Gareth Smythe was calling."

Isabelle nodded. "Please show Lord Smythe in and then ask the cook if we can have some refreshments."

When Gareth walked into the room, she could see the distress on his face. He walked towards her and took her hand in his.

"My goodness, Lady Isabelle, I'm at a loss to know what to say. The revenge that Zavier planned has gone so wrong. When he came up with the plan, I tried to dissuade him, to no avail, and when you overheard his argument with your mother, I pleaded with him to leave you alone.

I haven't talked to Zavier yet. All I have heard are the gossipers' version of events. Will you tell me what happened?"

Isabelle related the events of the evening, but when she got to the time the horde of people arrived at the library door, she frowned.

"Gareth, I guess Lord Fagean arrived at the library by eliminating the other doors in that hallway, but how did the society matrons and assorted sticky beaks find us? I could hear them as they advanced along the hallway, and they didn't look in any other rooms to find me; they came straight to the library. The only person who knew where I went was my mother."

Isabelle paused, and her face paled. She turned to look at Gareth.

"Dear God, my mother set up the whole thing to force Lord Fagean to marry me."

Gareth turned over the events in his mind and reached the same conclusion Isabelle had.

"Lady Isabelle..."

"Call me Isabelle; we're past the time when we need formalities. When he stormed out of the room, he shouted that the bitch had stolen his youth, and he didn't intend to let it happen again. Do you know the truth behind their feud?"

"Yes, but now you know enough to tackle your mother. Please, don't believe everything your mother tells you. She was in the wrong, and Zavier suffered because of her lies and accusations."

"Knowing what happened doesn't change my circumstances."

"You're right. What are you going to do? I considered asking you to marry me, but my mother thought the scandal would affect my sisters."

Isabelle grinned. "That was a very nice thought, but I will not marry. I will enter the Bakersville convent in a week or two."

"No, no, no. There must be an alternative."

"Gareth, I will not marry one of my mother's esteemed aristocrats, and no decent man will have me. My mother is eager to resolve the problem, and the convent seems the best option. The convent will give me the peace and care I want."

The door opened, and her mother said, "As if you aren't disgraced enough, you are entertaining a man without a chaperone. Do you never learn?"

Isabelle rose. "How much more can I be disgraced? I will willingly entertain Lord Smythe whenever he calls. Unlike the busybodies, Gareth called as a show of sympathy, and I appreciate his visit."

Isabelle asked Benz to show Gareth out and rounded on her mother.

"We need to discuss some facts which have come to light, and I want my father to hear what I have to say."

Lady Beaumont scoffed. "As if your father has time for your excuses and suppositions."

"In a week or two, I will be gone, and you can wash your hands of me then, but believe me, my father will make time to see me, and you need to be there."

As Isabelle entered her father's study, he lifted his head to acknowledge her. Clifford Beaumont noticed the expression of determination on his daughter, in contrast to the look of distaste on his wife's face. He hoped there would be no extra dramas to add to the traumatic week the family had endured, but suspected fate would deny his wish.

"Father, I have important information to discuss with you, and although Mother is reluctant to participate, I believe she needs to hear my revelation."

Lord Beaumont placed his pen on his blotter and indicated the seats before his desk.

"Why don't you ladies take a seat? Should I ask Benz for refreshments?"

"No, thank you. I have had morning tea with Lord Smythe. As you know, Lord Smythe is a friend of Lord Fagean, but he called to offer comfort and support. He asked me the truth of the incident because he hadn't seen Lord Fagean and only knew what the ton was saying. As I recalled the facts, he asked questions, and it became clear that your wife, my mother, alerted the old biddies who found Lord Fagean and me together."

Lord Beaumont glared at his wife. "Is this true, Hazel?"

Hazel Beaumont bristled and rose from her chair. "The accusation is preposterous. Why would I want society to know that the cad compromised her?"

Lord Beaumont queried his daughter. "Do you think you might be overreacting, Isabelle? What purpose would your mother have for shaming you in such a way?"

"Father, I have been the meat in the sandwich during my courtship. Lord Fagean and Mother hate each other so much that they have no concern for my feelings and reputation. My mother was the only person who knew where I went when I left the ballroom; she suggested I go to the library. I'm assuming Lord Fagean opened doors to see which room I was in, but the busybodies came straight to the library without opening and closing doors. We could hear their outraged voices as they walked along the corridor. Mother hoped to back Lord Fagean into a corner, so he had to offer for me, but it backfired."

"Dear me, I find it hard to imagine your mother placing you in this position. Why would she want Lord Fagean to offer for you when she hates him?"

"Because many years ago, Mother and Lord Fagean knew each other. I don't know all the details, but Lord Fagean's father banished him to the continent because of what happened between them. Lord Fagean's angry retort at the scandalised elders suggested that once before, Mother had tried to have him compromise her."

The silence in the room after Isabelle's announcement engulfed the occupants.

"When we married, Hazel, your father told me that you had suffered a traumatic experience, and I should be patient. You never wanted to discuss it, and I won't press the issue, but I fear you have punished Lord Fagan enough, and when it ruins my daughter, you have gone too far."

"Mother, Lord Fagean's father went to his grave believing his son was a debaucher of innocent women. How frightened Zavier must have felt when alone in a foreign country. On the other hand, you lived an ordinary life, marrying and having children, and the community held you in high esteem. Did you ever consider apologising to him or setting the record straight before his father died? It seems to me that he was justified in wanting revenge; I wish I hadn't been the collateral damage."

"Isabelle, now that you know how you came to be compromised, is there another way aside from the convent?"

"With or without the truth, my circumstances have not changed. I was undesirable as a bride when Lord Fagean shunned me, but after my mother attempted to manipulate him, I became the most unmarriageable debutante ever. Before Mother and Lord Fagean ruined me, I had very few friends; now, I have none. I need to disappear if you want to find husbands for Esme and Rose in a few years. I don't think I am brave enough to venture to the continent to find a husband. Living in the convent will be challenging, but at least there will be no people giving me the cut direct or women gossiping behind their fans as I walk past. No one will judge me at the convent, and I will have women surrounding me with warmth and kindness. It is the best I can hope for in my life."

She had told Gareth the same thing and hoped she might believe it if she repeated it enough times. Her future, confined to the convent, was almost like being imprisoned. She would leave her family and home behind when she walked through the convent doors. The truth hit her hard, and she scampered from the room rather than give her mother the satisfaction of watching her daughter cry.

Chapter Nine

While Isabelle prepared to leave for the convent, Lord Fagean swilled whisky and cursed the Beaumont women who had ruined his life. Long ago, Hazel Emmerson had cried rape and had him exiled to the continent, and then, years later, her daughter had destroyed his opportunity with Marie Dickerson, the American heiress. When his butler announced the arrival of Gareth Smyth, Zavier barely acknowledged his friend. He gaped in surprise when Gareth grabbed him by the shirt front and pulled him upright. Before Zavier could utter a word, Gareth punched him in the nose. As Zavier howled on the floor and frantically searched for his kerchief to slow the gush of blood from his nose, Gareth grabbed a glass and poured a large quantity of whisky.

Minutes later, when Gareth's temper subsided and Zavier's nose stopped bleeding, the two men regarded each other.

"What the hell was that for?"

"Isabelle's only option is to enter the convent in Bakerville. She will have no family life, ever. Her lot in life will be scrubbing floors, weeding gardens, and eating only what the sisters can grow in their gardens, while sleeping on a thin pad on the ground each night. Was your damned revenge worth it? You aimed to ruin Isabelle and succeeded beyond your wildest dreams, but you didn't succeed in upsetting her mother; the woman doesn't care. She focused on removing Isabelle from the public eye as quickly as possible. Why are you swilling whisky?"

"A convent? There must be some sad sap who would marry her."

"Of course, there's not unless she heads overseas, and then that's not a given. I considered marrying her, but my mother thinks the scandal will ruin my sisters' opportunities to make a good match next year."

"Well, what the heck? Isabelle ruined my chance with Marie Dickerson, the American heiress. She said she doesn't want a man with a title and a scandal attached to his name, so she isn't interested in me."

"So all you got out of the punch and our conversation is that Isabelle messed up your life? There will be other women for you to choose from, but for Isabelle, there is no future. You're a real cad, concerned only about how this affected you when you started the whole saga. Isabelle realised that her mother sent the old biddies and the society snobs to interrupt you. It's challenging to decide which one of you disgusts me more. I can't bear to be around you now, and I'm not sure how long my anger will last."

Gareth strode to the door, and before he could open it, the butler appeared and performed the task. Gareth quit the foyer with a curt nod and headed for his coach. How had he not noticed that his friend was self-centred and entitled? Gareth racked his brain for the entire journey to find Isabelle a suitor. Her family and society shouldn't relegate a beautiful young woman to a convent after her mother and a self-important cad destroyed her. Where was the punishment for the instigators of this debacle? Did nobody but him care what happened to Isabelle? As Gareth searched his brain for a likely candidate, feeling sorry for himself, Zavier continued to drink until the decanter held not a single drop, and he was well in his cups.

The following day, when Xavier opened his eyes, he found himself stretched out on the settee, having fallen asleep sometime during the night, covered by a blanket. His face hurt, and snippets of his argument with Gareth filtered through his tired brain. Zavier groaned as he rolled over and dragged himself off the sofa; it was time to clean up for the day ahead. As he staggered towards his room, his butler handed him a disgusting-looking concoction. From previous experience, Zavier knew that Mrs Covington's remedy for a hangover worked, but the trick was to swallow it in one go without gagging or regurgitating it.

After a bath and a change of clothes, Zavier considered his day. As he contemplated the entertainment for the day, he recalled the conversation with Gareth. His friend's announcement that if not for his sisters, he would marry Isabelle stuck in his craw. Could he see Isabelle frequently, attached to Gareth's arm, or her belly swollen as she carried Gareth's child? He thought he had reconciled himself to seeing Isabelle with a nameless suitor, but the thought of Isabelle with Gareth raised his hackles. What if Gareth found a husband for her, and he had to see the couple at social outings and business meetings? Remembering that Gareth said Isabelle's only option was a convent made him wince. He didn't want her, did he? Zavier sighed and ran a hand through his carefully coiffed hair. What would it be like to be married to Isabelle? The information Gareth gave him yesterday — that Isabelle had discovered her mother was the person who set the jackals on them — didn't surprise him. Zavier needed to track his friend down and discuss what they could do to prevent Isabelle from disappearing behind the convent walls, never to be seen in a ballroom again.

Calling for his carriage, Zavier headed for his friend's place. He hoped Gareth had control of his temper because he didn't want another punch in the nose. Even though his hangover had subsided, the pain Gareth's punch had caused hadn't diminished. When he entered his friend's house, he held up his hands in a surrender gesture.

"I came to see if we could find a suitor for Isabelle. I agree that she is a good person who doesn't deserve to retire to a convent. I tried to apologise the other night, but we were interrupted by her mother's posse. Let's make a list and see what we come up with."

An hour later, he and Gareth sat at his friend's desk, strewn with papers covered in names. The two men listed every man who wasn't courting a woman and discussed them as options. Some men were too old, others had gambling habits, and others were unlikely to be faithful husbands.

"Who knew there were so many undesirables in society? Do you know any men without titles? Maybe a merchant with good holdings who could keep Isabelle in comfort?"

Gareth shook his head. "I'm acquainted with a few but not well enough to ask them to marry Isabelle."

As they disregarded each man, it became clear that Zavier was the only person with a title, money and a functioning estate who fit the bill.

"Well, my friend, you were looking for a wife; it seems you found a prospective bride. How do you feel about marrying Isabelle? It's you or the convent."

"I can't believe it has come to this. I planned to ruin the girl to pay her mother back, and I never considered what would happen to the girl when I achieved my revenge. I like her, and I guess my only objection is that Beaumont cow will be my mother-in-law."

"After setting up Isabelle to be compromised, I doubt she would want to see her mother soon. You could live on your estate and never have to see her."

"Do you think she will think I'm a better option than the convent?"

"Probably not, but she said that her father was appalled at the suggestion of the convent, so it might be better to side-step Isabelle and go straight to him."

"That's a good thought, but there's one problem. The butler won't let me past the front door."

"Man up, Zavier. You lived alone on the continent for nearly eighteen years and managed to survive. Talk your way into the house. I'll organise a meeting tomorrow if you can't get past the butler today. We don't have much time before her mother packs her off to the convent and washes her hands of Isabelle."

Zavier took a deep breath and said, "Wish me luck."

Surprisingly, the butler allowed Zavier to enter the house and escorted him towards Lord Beaumont's study. Once Zavier entered the room, Lord Beamont's genial expression disappeared, and a look of pure hatred replaced it.

"What the devil are you doing here? How did you get past, Benz? I'll fire that man for letting trash like you into my home."

"He let me in because he doesn't want Isabelle to disappear into a convent, never allowing her to have a family or a home of her own."

Lord Beaumont sneered. "And why should that concern you? If I'm not mistaken, you engineered this whole catastrophe."

"Yes, I set the ball in motion, but your wife ruined your daughter entirely by trying to force me to marry the chit. It's the same damned trick the woman pulled on me, and I was too angry that she caught me again to consider what my refusal would mean for Isabelle. Your wife ruined my life. She told her father that I had forced myself on her, and the truth was that she arrived in my bedroom naked, hoping that someone would see us, and when I bolted from the room and spent the night in the servant's quarters, she ran to her father and told him lies. I concede that I went about getting revenge the wrong way, and I injured Isabelle, which I regret. But if you agree, I will marry her. I can give her a family and a comfortable life. The thought of her scrubbing floors in the convent makes me shudder."

"What makes you think Isabelle will agree to marry you?"

Zavier grinned. "I'm sure she won't, but if you and I sign a marriage agreement, she will have no choice. I'm confident she will come around once we return to my estate."

Chapter Ten

Breaking the news to the family, particularly Isabelle, was a task Lord Beaumont didn't relish. After Lord Fagean's visit, questions regarding his marriage to Hazel were foremost in his mind. The Duke insisted that the accusations Hazel made against him when she was a young woman were untrue, and discovering that Hazel was a maiden when they married proved that she had made false claims. The consequences of her claims ruined the young Fagean's future, and he couldn't understand her refusal to acknowledge that she had made a mistake. Clifford Beaumont pushed his questions aside; there would be time enough to question his wife after he announced Isabelle's betrothal. Lord Fagean was to acquire a special licence, and the two would be married tomorrow morning.

His wife raised her head from her embroidery when he entered the room. As he made his way to the settee, he said,

"Ladies, I have had a visitor in my study for the last hour or two, and I'm pleased to say I have signed a marriage contract for Isabelle."

Isabell shot from her seat. "No, I won't marry some aging fool you managed to bribe."

Clifford Beaumont smiled at Isabelle. "Oh, yeah, of little faith. I would never sell you to some ancient old fool who recently decided he needs an heir. Your bridegroom is Lord Fagean."

Isabelle flopped into a chair as her mother's smile of satisfaction covered her face.

"Now you can thank me for making him step up after he compromised you, Isabelle."

Isabelle burst into tears. "Now I will be married to a man who hates me, and all I feel for him is contempt."

Lord Beaumont crossed the room to sit next to Isabelle.

"My dear, he doesn't hate you. The thought of you scrubbing floors and living in a convent brought him to his senses. He said the other night when he refused, it was because your mother had tried that trick when he was a young man, and when it failed, she lied about his behaviour towards her."

An outraged cry came from Hazel Beaumont. "How can you say such outrageous things? The man is a liar and a cad."

"This conversation should be private, but because it affects Isabelle's life, I will forget etiquette for a moment and say that on our wedding night, I discovered you were a maiden."

Isabelle blushed but kept her attention on her father.

Lord Beaumont continued. "If Lord Fagean had forced himself on you, which was what you told your father, then you wouldn't have been a maiden when we married."

Isabelle glared at her mother.

"Good heavens, mother. You falsely accused him of heinous crimes, and his father disowned him. He lived overseas for eighteen years, and now, after all your warnings to me, you are the culprit."

Lady Beaumont lashed out.

"He bedded anything that lay down for him: widows, unhappily married ladies, tavern wenches and sometimes even the maids. But he wouldn't touch me. I was twenty-three, and after two unsuccessful seasons, I thought I'd never marry, so I wanted to know what all the giggles and blushes were about. When he discovered me, he looked revolted and bolted for the door. One of the house guests caught me leaving his room, and I needed him to offer for me, but he didn't return that night, so I made up a story and told my father in the morning."

Lord Beaumont shook his head. "I'm lost for words. It's time you let go of your contempt for a man who did the honourable thing. There is no way to restore his lost years, but you need to work on an apology, especially as he will be your son-in-law by tomorrow afternoon."

"Father, even knowing what Mother did, he treated me with a lack of care and concern, and now he feels guilty for calling my reputation into question. I can't marry him under those circumstances."

"I'm sorry, Isabelle, but the documents are signed; by tomorrow, Fagean will have a special licence, and you will marry in the parlour. It might be wise to warn your maid that your plans have changed, and you need all your belongings packed."

Isabelle surveyed the stack of luggage on the floor of her bedroom. Bessie was organised and efficient, and it saddened Isabelle to know that her good friend and lady's maid was not making the journey to Lord Ragean's estate. Isabelle knew nothing about Ragean's estate, not even how far away the holding was. Isabelle would much rather stay in town, but the ton would be unkind even with her marriage, and the scandal her mother and the Duke caused would never fade from the memory of the vindictive ladies who ruled society.

Tomorrow, she would marry a man she detested, and their forced marriage didn't give her thoughts of a happy life ahead. She and the Duke would be locked in a marriage that neither wanted, and while she detested him, she was sure he held the same sentiments regarding her.

Her sisters, too young to understand the undercurrents surrounding their parents and Isabelle, were excited about her wedding but unhappy to hear that their big sister would leave her childhood home to make a life in another part of the county. Esme and Rose sighed over Isabelle's handsome future husband and wanted to deck her out in her finest for the ceremony. The two girls had coerced the gardener into picking blooms for a posy for Isabelle to hold during the marriage service. Isabelle didn't want to disillusion her sisters, but even the bouquet was more festive than Isabelle wanted. She hoped her sisters would one day find good and decent men to marry them. Her eyes teared up as Isabelle realised that even with her marriage to Lord Ragean, her chances of returning to town were unlikely. Would she be able to attend her sister's weddings? Would she ever know her nieces or nephews? The scandal would stay with her throughout her life, and none of the old biddies who ruled the ton would ever forget. Was it uncharitable of her to hope for their early demise? But even if they all died, there would be another gaggle of nasty old biddies to take their places.

Chapter Eleven

I sabelle walked the short distance to the front of the room, where her groom waited. Lord Ragean stood facing the minister without even glancing to the side to acknowledge her as her father deposited her at his side and stepped away. The ceremony was brief, and when the minister announced they were man and wife, Isabelle wept quietly throughout the service. The staff member who witnessed the marriage stepped forward to wish her well before returning to their duties. After she said goodbye, the newly married couple headed for the carriage parked at the entrance of the house. Lord Ragean helped Isabelle into the carriage, and once he was seated, he wrapped the roof, and the vehicle started.

As they drove down the driveway, Isabelle felt her mood worsen; was the silence he was treating her with normal for their marriage? Lord Fagean had not spoken to her at all today except for the words I do. Were they going to sit in silence for the length of the journey? The tears Isabelle shed during the ceremony flooded her eyes again, and she turned her head towards the window so her new husband couldn't see the depth of her despair.

After travelling silently for hours, the day's tension caught up with Isabelle, and she closed her eyes. If her travelling companion had attempted to converse with her, she might have conceded that they couldn't conduct their marriage in silence and answered him, but the man said nothing. In her dream-like state, Isabelle thought the carriage had stopped, but by the time she considered asking what was happening, she felt the motion of the carriage resume, and she dozed off again.

When Isabelle awoke, the fast-fading light she could see from the window indicated that she had slept most of the day away, and she wondered how close they were to their destination. She turned to ask Zavier, only to discover she was alone in the carriage. Panic gripped her. Where was her husband? Did he intend to leave her somewhere along the route? Isabelle pulled the curtains aside and looked out of the window. There was nothing to see but vast open fields and the barren road they traversed. Scooting to the other side of the carriage, Isabelle pulled back the curtains, and panic gripped her when she could see no riders—had her new husband abandoned her to the care of a driver? She knew he didn't want to marry her, and if this solitary ride were his idea of providing a better life for her, she would gladly scrub floors and sleep on a pallet on the floor at the convent.

The driver slowed the horses and pulled them to a stop. Isabelle felt the bile rise in her throat. What was the man going to do to her? When nothing happened, she wondered what was happening, and she peered out the window to see the man buttoning his falls and walking towards the carriage. Isabelle needed to ask where her husband was, but didn't know if the driver was trustworthy. Removing one of the long pins that had secured her hair in place, Isabelle held the only weapon she had at her disposal and called out,

"Coachman, where are my husband and the other men escorting our carriage?"

The man walked to the window and bobbed his head.

"The master and the outriders have gone ahead because we are on Lord Fagean's land, and there should be no need for the outriders. We should reach the manor house before dark, my lady."

"Thank you."

Isabelle was angry that Lord Fagean had left the driver and her to their own devices while he and his outriders were probably already eating dinner and relaxing. Relieved that the driver wouldn't abandon her on the road or murder her in the carriage, Isabelle settled back and watched as the flat, uninspiring landscape flashed past. A loud crack startled Isabelle, and as the carriage lurched to the side, she felt the carriage horses surge. The carriage pitched to one side, and the movement slammed Isabelle into the wall. When her head hit the edge of the seat, she slumped, and the tumbling vehicle tossed her unconscious body around like a rag doll. While the driver tried to control the frantic horses, they towed the stricken carriage on its side along the uneven roadway. Regaining consciousness, Isabelle felt blood trickle down her face. The carriage was careening along on its side, and Isabelle had nothing to anchor herself to prevent her from being thrown around. Never before had Isabelle felt so frightened, and when the carriage came to a halt, she let out a shuddering sigh. When Isabelle discovered what felt like a large gash on her forehead, she could do nothing to stop the blood. As she pulled herself to a sitting position, she realised that the carriage lay sideways, with the door against the ground. How was she supposed to get out of the carriage?

"Lady Fagean, are you injured?"

"I am alive, but I need help to get out of here. The door is against the road."

Isabelle heard the coachman swear.

"I'm afraid the horses may bolt again if I leave them. I'll try engaging the brake and see what happens."

After some banging and clattering, Isabelle saw the diver lean in from the broken window above her, which was her only means of escape. She raised her hands, and the driver gripped her wrists and pulled her through the window. When he lowered Isabelle to the ground, the driver shook his head. Where some ladies would be wailing and weeping, Lady Fagean controlled herself. In the waning light, John the coachman could see a nasty gash on Isabelle's forehead, blood from her wound trickling down her face, and bruises beginning to bloom on her cheeks. As she moved away from the carriage, she staggered and limped, so he knew she had other injuries apart from those on her face.

"I might need to leave you here, and I'll ride one of the horses to the house for help."

Despite the ache in her head, Isabelle refused to be left behind.

"Oh, no, you don't. If you boost me up, I will ride the other horse. It's nearly night and will be as dark as pitch in another half hour."

"Ah, riding side saddle on a carriage horse with no saddle will be dangerous, my lady."

"You are right, which is why I will ride astride. Unhook the horses from the traces and help me on. The sooner we leave, the sooner we will arrive at the house. The repairs can wait until tomorrow, and I'll manage without my trunks for one night."

The horses were agitated, and Isabelle's mount took exception to her dress, shying and skittering away from her voluminous skirts. She tucked the skirts underneath her, and finally, her mount settled into a pace-eating walk. John Coachman kept a close eye on Isabelle, not wanting to have her further injure herself by swooning and falling off the horse. Isabelle stayed close to the driver in the falling light, afraid of getting lost on this deserted roadway.

The long ride to the manor house was a blur for Isabelle; her head thumped, and she felt dizzy and nauseous. Where the hell were they going? Surely the house was close? It seemed like she and John Coachman had ridden for hours, and her determination to stay upright on this mammoth horse wavered. When John announced they had arrived, Isabelle wondered how he could see anything. As Isabelle peered through the darkness, she thought she saw the outline of the entrance, but no lights showed there or in the house. Eager to end this journey, Isabelle eased her legs to the horse's side as John called out.

"Wait, Lady Fagaen, and I will help you."

Isabelle nodded, happy to wait for the driver, but before he reached her, she slid forward and crumpled onto the ground.

With a cry of distress, John raced to catch the Duchess, but his attempt was to no avail, and he looked down at the unconscious form of his mistress. John lifted Isabelle and carried her to the main door. Balancing his mistress and hammering on the door caused John to jiggle Isabelle, but when there was no response to his knocking, he cursed and headed towards the rear of the house to enter through the scullery. As he turned the handle and shoved the door, startled faces turned to him.

"Stop staring, you cretins and help me. Lady Isabelle needs medical attention."

The butler was the first to regain his senses, and he snapped orders as John walked further into the room carrying his mistress.

"Ruthie, show John to the room we prepared for her ladyship and you two," he said, pointing at the footman, "need to carry hot water to the room. Mrs Hopkins, collect your medical supplies and find smelling salts, too."

As the staff swung into action, many questions arose among those not directly involved in Isabelle's immediate treatment about her unexpected arrival. When Lord Fagean and the outriders appeared some hours ago, they did not mention the carriage following them. There must have been an accident, as evidenced by the Duchess's prone form, but until John came back into the kitchen, the accident and its cause would remain a mystery. The butler, Andrews, dithered about the advisability of waking Lord Fagean. If he woke his master after the man had given strict instructions not to be disturbed, would he be subjected to the man's wrath? Lord Fagean's edict that he not be bothered meant that his master didn't want to know when his wife arrived, so Andrews decided to let the man sleep. He hoped the decision didn't cause more trouble than waking his master would.

As Ruthie and Mrs Hopkins removed Isabelle's dress, the welts and the beginnings of bruises on her body caused them to groan in sympathy. Once they laid Isabelle on the bed, Mrs Hopkins waved the smelling salts under her nose, and Isabelle groaned before averting her face.

"Wake up, my lady."

Isabelle opened her eyes, her disorientation clear to her nurses.

"You are at Lord Fagean's estate, my lady."

Isabelle nodded in understanding, but winced when the movement caused her throbbing headache to intensify.

"We need to clean your wounds, but are there others apart from those on your arms and legs?"

"I think I banged my head when the carriage tipped."

Mrs Hopkins ran her fingers through Isabelle's hair until her fingers felt the egg-like bump on her head.

"Do you have a headache?"

"Yes, it is so bad."

Mrs Hopkins and Ruthie got to work with warm, wet clothes and gentle fingers. The gash on Isabelle's forehead had long ago stopped weeping, and after they cleaned the dried blood, Mrs Hopkins covered it with a small bandage.

"Is John Coachman all right?"

"Yes, my lady, he is. I think a little laudanum might help you sleep."

Isabelle didn't care what the woman gave her as long as the throbbing in her head stopped.

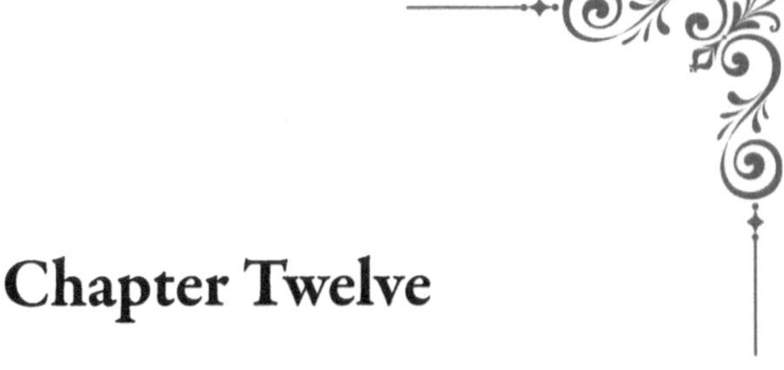

Chapter Twelve

I sabelle convinced Ruthie that she was well enough to leave her bed the second day after her arrival. The bruises on her body ached, but the headache had dissipated, and Isabelle was tired of her own company and the bedroom's four walls. As she entered the breakfast room, she saw her husband for the first time since he had abandoned the coach. Without looking at her, he landed his first barb.

"Huh, you've finally stopped sulking."

He glanced up from his paper and then did a double-take when he saw her face.

"What the devil happened to you?"

Isabelle glared at the man.

"As if you don't know."

"Damnation, woman, I wouldn't ask if I already knew."

Isabelle curled her lip as she looked at the man who was supposed to have saved her from scrubbing floors.

"I find it hard to believe you aren't kept up-to-date with the goings on at your estate. Although silly me, John Coachman and I were barely on your estate when you and those damned out riders bolted for the house and abandoned us to our own devices. I hope you had a nice meal and a restful sleep."

Zavier glared at the butler.

"Andrews, if my wife wants to talk in riddles, she may, but I want an explanation of how she came by those bruises."

"When you and the outriders arrived and didn't mention your wife, I assumed something had gone wrong with the wedding. You further confirmed that assumption when you retired and said you didn't want to be disturbed."

"Well, that doesn't explain anything."

"The carriage lost a wheel about an hour from here, and Lady Isabelle was knocked unconscious. When she came to, she was trapped in the coach, and John had trouble extracting her. When he brought the horses under control, he wasn't sure if they would stand, and there was no one to hold their heads. The mistress and John rode the carriage horses back, but Lady Isabelle swooned when they reached your front door, which I locked because we weren't expecting visitors. John carried the mistress to the back door and entered through the scullery."

While Andrews related the events of the night she arrived, Isabelle ignored her husband as she ate a hearty breakfast.

"Why the hell didn't you call me when John Coachman arrived with Isabelle?"

Andrews blushed, but his expression remained as stoic as ever.

"I didn't notify you, my Lord, because you had said you didn't wish to be disturbed, even though you knew your new bride was arriving. I assumed her welfare wasn't of concern to you, so the staff and I treated her ladyship."

As Zavier sat with his mouth open, Isabelle rose and thanked the staff for breakfast.

"Andrews, will you inform Mrs Hopkins that I would like a tour of the house, and could you organise for me to meet the staff? And please, could you direct me to the stables? I assume that is where I will find John Coachman?"

"I will accompany you."

"That's not necessary, my Lord. I'm sure you are far too busy to worry about my welfare."

Zavier growled. "I said I will accompany you."

The walk to the stables was silent; Isabelle wondered why Zavier bothered to accompany her when he had abandoned her two nights ago. When they reached the stables, Isabelle looked around with interest. Four horses poked their heads out of their stalls, and Isabelle smiled; she hoped one of these mounts would accept a side saddle. A man approached, his face surly until he noticed Zavier, and his features changed. Isabelle tucked that information away to think about later, but for now, she wanted to see John. Zavier spoke to the man and introduced Isabelle to him. She discovered the man's name was Bender, and she wasn't sure if that was his first or last name.

"Can you tell me where to find John? I wish to have a word with him."

Zavier shook his head. "Lady Isabelle is not traipsing through the stables looking for the coachman. Send a stable hand to find him."

As she waited for John to arrive, Isabelle scanned the area. The stalls looked clean, and the tack hanging on the walls was clean, with the brass buckles gleaming in the morning light. When John arrived, she stepped towards him and welcomed him with a smile.

"I had to see you to thank you for all you did for me after the wheel came off the carriage. I thought I would die, but then you pulled me out of the window. I'm sorry I passed out and you had to carry me, but I wanted to tell you how grateful I am that you were with me."

John ducked his head, and Isabelle thought nobody showed appreciation for a job well done in the stables or the estate if he was bashful at receiving thanks for his deeds.

John looked up at Isabelle and said. "Helping you was my pleasure, Lady Isabelle. I hope the bruising fades quickly."

Bender interrupted the two, saying, "You need to get moving, coachman. The other conveyances require checking to see that an accident doesn't happen to anyone else."

As they walked back to the house, Zavier said in a clipped voice, "Was that necessary?"

"I told you not to accompany me, but you insisted. What did you think I wanted to say to the coachman? He helped while you languished in bed, my Lord. Of course, I would thank him."

Zavier grunted and walked quickly to the door, leaving her in his wake.

Isabelle didn't see Zavier again that day, dining alone in the cavernous dining room. As the days passed, Isabelle wondered if Zavier was still at the estate or had left her to return to town. Her thoughts of avoiding Zavier were unnecessary, as he successfully distanced himself from he

A week after her arrival, Isabelle decided that if Zavier didn't intend to show himself, she would take the run-down estate in hand and make changes where she wished. The first change she planned to make was to her sleeping arrangements. The night of her arrival, the housekeeper placed her in one of the guest rooms, not the Duchess's rooms. With determination, Isabelle walked to the kitchen, looking for Mrs Hopkins. The woman sat at the table with the cook, and the women shot to their feet when Isabelle appeared.

"Lady Isabelle, I was just..."

"Mrs Hopkins, Cookie, I am not such an ogre that I would deprive you of a break. Take your time, but I'll be in the sitting room when you're ready. I have some repairs to a dress that will keep me busy for a while."

Isabelle sat in the sitting room, and rather than mend the small tear in her dress, she scanned the room. After the housekeeper gave Isabelle a tour of the house when she arrived, it was evident that the late Duke had not changed a thing since the dowager Duchess died. When Zavier married her, he said he didn't need her dowry to bolster the estate's coffers, so Isabelle decided to use the money to revamp the tired decor in the house. As Isabelle visualised the changes she could make in this room, Mrs Hopkins arrived.

"Ah, Mrs Hopkins, please come and join me. Can you tell me why I am sleeping in a guest room, not the Duchess's?"

Mrs Hopkins nodded. "The late Duke refused to change anything when his wife died, and he instructed us to close up her room. He forbade us from cleaning the room, so I shudder to think what it looks like after ten years."

"And has my husband given any instructions about that room?"

"No, my Lady, he hasn't."

"I have no intentions of remaining in a guest room, so we should look at the state of the Duchess's rooms and do some cleaning. It might be best for you and me to check the room before we start cleaning; it will give us an idea of how badly the room has deteriorated."

When Mrs Hopkins used her keys to unlock the door, Isabelle held her breath. The two women looked at each other, and then Mrs Hopkins pushed the door open. Isabelle gasped in disbelief; the room was a shambles. The late Duke may have quarantined this room, but only after he had destroyed it. In his rage or grief, the late Duke wrecked the furniture and the fittings. A mirror, which appeared to be part of the Duchess's dressing table, was shattered into a million pieces, and the material hangings around the bed had large slashes.

"Now I know why he refused to let us dust and mop. What do you want to do, Lady Isabelle?"

"We need the footmen to remove the broken furniture, and then the maids need to cover their hair and bring brooms, mops and cloths. When you call the footmen, please ask Ruthie to come to my room. I need to change my dress and cover my hair if I am to help you."

Once she changed and donned a headscarf, Isabelle investigated the dressing room that housed the Duchess's clothes. To her amazement, Isabelle discovered that the room was filled with clothes, and further investigation revealed drawers of undergarments and shoes. As a maid packed the undergarments and shoes in a trunk, Isabelle and Mrs Hopkins gathered armfuls of dresses to place on the bed in the guest room closest to the Duchess's rooms. The noise of a carriage didn't deter Isabelle from her task; if he husband decided to bless her with his presence, then greeting him would be unnecessary.

The sudden noise of arguing was Isabelle's first sign that the carriage was not her husband returning from wherever he was hiding. Isabelle glanced at Mrs Hopkins, and the two women, leaving the maids to clean, ventured into the hallway. Two women were directing the footmen and arguing with Andrews.

"Andrews, what is happening, and who are these women?"

"Lady Isabelle, these two ladies are Lord Fagean's sisters. There is a problem because you are in the room Lady Pettigrew usually uses."

Isabelle scrutinised the women.

"Forgive me, ladies, but the notice of your arrival didn't reach us. I am sorry if I am currently sleeping in a room you use, but I'm certain that Mrs Hopkins will be able to settle you in another room."

The woman she was speaking to sneered at Isabelle.

"We didn't notify you of our arrival because this is our home. You fail to understand; that's my room, and you must move."

"Before we discuss this further, I believe an introduction wouldn't go astray. Mrs Hopkins, will you ask Cookie for refreshments? We will take this conversation into the sitting room. Ladies, if you want to join me, we can sort out the problem."

The disgruntled women followed Isabelle and had barely taken their seats when they began their tirade. Refusing to be drawn into a battle with these women, Isabelle said.

"Forgive me, but my husband has never spoken of his sisters, so your arrival is startling. Could you please introduce yourselves?"

With bad grace, the women introduced themselves. The more vocal woman was Lady Esme Pettigrew, and her sister was Lady Elizabeth Blackmore. While Isabelle remained calm on the surface, she was seething underneath. How dare these women arrive unannounced a week after she and Zavier married?

"Thank you for the introduction. I'm interested to know about your family. Are you both married with children? Are your husbands still alive and living with you?"

Lady Esme snorted. "We are married to living husbands, and I have two children, and Elizabeth has three children. Now you are all caught up; we want to settle in our rooms."

"You said in the foyer that you arrive whenever you please because this is your home. Did I hear that correctly?"

"Are you simple? Did Zavier marry an idiot? "

"My intellect is not the subject here, but understand this: your father, God rest his soul, may have been happy for you to arrive and stay for long periods, but I am not. Your homes are where your husbands and children live, not this place where you grew up. This house is now Zavier's home; as his wife, it is mine. Your unannounced arrival is not polite, and as the staff and I are currently refurbishing the duchess's room, I am sleeping in the room closest to the master suite. You will not be able to sleep in the room you generally use, and your stay will be of short duration."

Elizabeth Blackmore surged from her seat in a most unladylike manner. "You have no right to enter my mother's suite. My Father had the room closed because it was too painful for him to see it empty, and we will not allow you to desecrate her memory by removing her presence from that room."

"My refurbishment can cause your father no more grief. I have finished talking to you two, but you have a choice. Either sleep in the rooms Mrs Hopkins assigns you or at the nearest inn."

"Where is Zavier? You are the intruder, and this place is our birthright. We will not tolerate you telling us what to do in our home. Our brother will not let you order us around."

"Where Zavier is hiding is anyone's guess, but until you can grumble to him, I suggest you retire to your rooms. I am weary of your complaints."

Isabelle walked to the door.

"Andrews, please ask Mrs Hopkins to show these women to their rooms. If their accommodation is unsatisfactory, ask the footmen to load their trunks on their carriage, and they can spend the night at the nearest inn. Oh, and if you know of my husband's whereabouts, it is time he returned to straighten out this problem."

Chapter Thirteen

As Andrews announced dinner, Zavier descended the stairs with his sisters. Despite her ongoing anger with Zavier, Isabelle was happy to see him. She hated to admit that she missed him, and dressed for dinner in an impeccable suit, she realised again how handsome he was. Watching him escort his sisters to the table sent a surge of jealousy through Isabelle. He should have accompanied his wife, not the trouble-making sisters. When Andrews pulled out her chair, she smiled and thanked her. Standing at the table, looking like a fool while Zavier fussed over his sister, took the glow off her appreciation at seeing him. Isabelle sat opposite Zavier, and as she watched him instruct Andrews to send in the food, she realised that he was out of her league. While he had courted her, Isabelle got caught up in the pleasure of his attention and the exciting places he took her. Now, however, she realised he was far more sophisticated than she, and she was just as he described her: young and foolish.

Zavier covertly watched his bride as he escorted his sisters from their room to the table. He thought she looked pleased to see him, even though she only inclined her head when he passed her. He cursed himself for leaving her standing at the end of the table, and her gratitude to Andrews showed how awkward and foolish she felt. Her scrutiny of him caused him to wonder if she missed him, but once she was seated at the table, her face became sombre, and her eyes dulled. Zavier quietly cursed. He had assured her father he could wear down her anger at the forced marriage, but they had had a spat, and he left the estate for almost a week. If he continued to upset Isabelle, he would never be able to soothe her anger. His sister's unwelcome appearance had added to the strain between them, and he wanted nothing more than to wrap his arms around her and hold her until her anger dissipated.

While Zavier's mind juggled with his and Isabelle's difficulties, she firmly fixed her thoughts on the problem. Isabelle hoped Zavier could set his sisters right about whose home this was. The meal was mostly silent, although her husband and his sisters exchanged pleasantries. Zavier asked about his nephews and niece, as well as the health of their spouses. Isabelle doubted that the two women would argue while the servants were present, but she knew they had not accepted her proclamations.

At the end of the meal, Zavier suggested the company retire to the parlour and asked Andrews to have the housekeeper serve tea. When they poured the cups and the servant left, Lady Esme listed her grievances to Zavier. She reiterated the earlier arguments about this being their childhood home and their desire to arrive when the fancy took them. Lady Esme complained about being unable to sleep in her bedroom, and before she could complain about the duchess's rooms, her sister raised her voice. Lady Elizabeth wailed about Isabelle desecrating their mother's memory and insisted that Zavier take his wife in hand.

Isabelle had never been good at reading Zavier's expressions, and now was no different. Even during their fake courtship, he rarely relaxed his expression and had his emotions firmly under control. She had only once seen him lose his temper in that ugly argument with her mother. Would he side with his sisters or back his wife? Would his recent avoidance of her not augur well for his support? Isabell waited with bated breath.

"It seems we have a problem, and I think it would be wise to sleep on the issues and further decide on a solution tomorrow. There is no sense in making rash decisions when we are tired. After your long journey, ladies, I imagine you are exhausted. Retire now, and we will discuss this problem tomorrow."

Zavier's sisters grumbled at their brother's decision but abided by it with bad grace. When her husband escorted his sisters from the room, Isabelle felt the sting of rejection once again. His absence since the spat about her thanking John for helping her had unsettled Isabelle. Was Zavier going to disappear every time they argued? More importantly, where did he go? Did he have a mistress he visited, or was it some random woman? As she walked to the guest room, she wondered if Zavier would talk to her before deciding on his sisters' complaints or if he would make a ducal decree that she had to abide by. The answer to the last question came sooner than expected.

Zavier tapped on the door to his wife's room, and when she opened it, he entered without comment.

"What can I do for you, my Lord?"

"Would I be right in assuming my sisters and you argued about their unannounced arrival and belief that this house is their home?"

"Yes, you would be right. We also argued about my refurbishing your mother's rooms for my use."

"Why are you refurbishing my mother's rooms?"

"I refuse to sleep in a guest bedroom when I am the Duchess. I have no intention of being the laughingstock of the ton when it becomes evident that my husband never visits my bed."

Zavier sighed. "Can we discuss that later? For the moment, it might be prudent to humour my sisters. They are upset about my father's death and find comfort in returning to their childhood home."

"So tomorrow, you will tell them they can arrive without notice whenever the urge grabs them? I must vacate this room and stop using the Duchess suite for my own purposes. Is that what you are telling me? Which guest bedroom do you suggest I use?"

Zavier looked uncomfortable, but Isabelle had more restraint than his sisters, so he'd rather deal with her ire than theirs.

"I'm sorry, but I don't know how to diffuse the situation. If arriving at random times was their practice when my father was alive, it will take a while for them to realise that they are intruding on our privacy. Until then, we will need to humour them."

"Humouring your sisters will affect the staff and me. Conversely, you will remove yourself to your study, and their outrageous comments and criticism will not touch you. The servants are taking the brunt of their anger, so don't be surprised when they find other jobs."

Isabelle watched her husband with an expressionless face. He cursed his sisters for putting him in this position; just when he thought he might be able to change Isabelle's belief that this was a marriage of convenience, he had to fail her again. The first morning Zavier had seen her injuries, he realised his negligence was to blame, and her stoicism and refusal to be beaten by the hand fate had dealt her caused a warm feeling in his chest. He realised with alarm that he cared for this stubborn young woman, even though he had resisted it all through their courtship.

Isabelle's declaration pulled his thoughts away from the disaster of his marriage to the measures she would take to follow his directions.

"I will change bedrooms in the morning and ask Mrs Hopkins to lock your mother's bedroom, but someone needs to disabuse your sisters of their romantic belief that your father asked Mrs Hopkins to lock the room and keep the staff out because of his grief. The real reason, which Mrs Hopkins and I discovered when we opened the room, was that your father destroyed the room. He slashed the linens and curtains, broke the furniture and smashed the mirror that graced your mother's dressing table. My Lord, your father demolished the room and didn't want anyone to know."

Zavier's face registered shock. "Surely not?"

Isabelle shrugged. "If you don't believe me, ask Mrs Hopkins or one of the footmen who carried out the destroyed furnishings."

The next day, Isabelle asked Mrs Hopkins and her maid to move her belongings to the guest room at the end of the long hallway. Leaving the ladies to their task, Isabelle entered the breakfast room. From the blank expressions on the server's faces, she surmised that the horrid women were already making complaints about the meal, the service, or anything else they could find that offended them. Gritting her teeth, Isabelle greeted her sisters-in-law, and the lack of reply was as she anticipated. Conor, the server, collected a plate and asked Isabelle what she would like for breakfast. Once he had filled her plate, he placed it before her and poured a cup of tea. As Conor stepped away, Lady Esme banged her fist on the tabletop.

"Boy, don't you think it is your job to serve all your betters, not just the woman masquerading as a Duchess?"

Conor swallowed convulsively, collected a plate for the woman, and politely enquired about her meal choices.

"For goodness' sake, just fill the plate."

When Connor placed the plate on the table, Lady Esme turned up her nose.

"Look at this rubbish that Zaverier's wife serves her guests for breakfast. You," she said, pointing at Conor, "should know my tastes by now. How dare you dish up this rubbish?"

Isabell had heard enough; she hated that the women looked down on her, but she refused to let them run roughshod over her staff.

"Conor, please collect the plate from Lady Esme's setting, and then you and the other servers may retire."

The sheer relief on Conor's face assured her that she had made the right decision. Isabelle began eating, and the silence in the room was ominous. When the explosion came, it did not surprise her; these women were the most entitled shrews she had the misfortune to meet, and as Isabelle had sent the servers away if they wanted to eat, they had to dish it themselves.

"Now that you have sent the servers away, how are we supposed to get our meal?"

Lady Elizabeth's question was so pathetic that Isabelle laughed.

"You dish the food yourself. I'm sure somewhere in your entitled lives, you have managed to dish food onto a plate. If you can't handle that task, I suggest you treat my staff with more respect in future."

Isabelle left the table and walked towards the kitchen, where the staff assembled.

"Andrews, please don't send the servers in to clean the breakfast room until those intolerable women have left."

"Yes, my lady. Can I be forward enough to ask how long Lord Fagean's sister will be here?"

"Lord Fagean thinks we should humour them, and from what I saw this morning, their presence here will affect the staff and me more than it will him. I will make myself scarce today, and I suggest you avoid them whenever possible."

"When the Duke died, we thought the random visits that caused us so much stress would stop. If these visits continue as they have for the last few years, the staff will be looking for new positions."

"I honestly don't blame anyone who wants to leave, but before you take drastic action, explain to Lord Fagaen what is happening."

Andrews took Lady Isabelle's suggestion and decided to notify Zavier of the staff's intention to find positions elsewhere as soon as the servers finished cleaning up after breakfast. He was grateful to Lady Isabelle for removing the young footman and the other servers from the breakfast room. Still, with Lord Fagean's sisters criticising and harassing his staff, the younger members made mistakes, giving the women more grounds for complaint. The situation couldn't continue, and he felt confident that Lord Fagean didn't know the seriousness of the problem.

Andrews hesitated before knocking on the study door. Even though Lord Fagean had been in residence for more than a year, he was still an unknown quantity regarding his temper. Would the man bluster and ignore his warnings as his father had, or would Lord Fagean take the staff situation seriously? As he entered the room, Andrews noted the complete lack of paperwork that adorned the old Duke's desk, and this spoke to a level of organisation in the young Duke that had been absent in his father.

Zavier lifted his head to see his butler waiting patiently before his desk.

"What can I do for you, Andrews?"

"Your grace, I believe it is my duty to inform you that many of the staff members here are contacting relatives and friends and attempting to secure new positions. When your father died, God rest his soul, we assumed that the unannounced visits from your sisters would cease. As this is not the case, many people are seeking new employment opportunities. We find Lady Pettigrew and Lady Blackwood challenging to work for, and the constant criticism and complaints cause nervousness amongst the staff, which leads to mistakes. Mistakes made by the staff lead to more complaints, which is an unending cycle."

Zavier sighed.

"I'm sorry, Andrews, but I feel that my sisters' desire to return to their childhood home is helping them to deal with their grief after losing our father. I can't evict them, but I'm sure they won't stay much longer. Can we be patient for the time being?"

Andrew's face remained stoic as he bowed to Lord Fagean and took his leave.

When the door clicked shut, Zavier rose from his chair and walked to the windows that overlooked the gardens. His sigh reflected the anger he felt. After years abroad, he had returned to do his duty, so why did he have to solve unnecessary problems? Would the staff quit? Most of the servants were long-time retainers, so he doubted the truth of Andrews' statement. Shrugging his shoulders, he pushed the conversation with the butler from his mind and returned to the never-ending pile of paperwork hidden in the drawers of the large desk.

Chapter Fourteen

Isabelle heard shouting and curses ringing from the sitting room. With a frown, she turned to her maid.

" Mrs Hopkins, what on earth is happening?"

"Lady Blackmore found dust behind a curtain, and she and Lady Pettigrew are shouting about the lack of cleanliness in the house."

"I am at my wits' end. Ask Andrews to meet me in the parlour."

When a frazzled butler arrived, the plan Isabelle had devised during the early morning hours was ready to be implemented.

"Andrews, this situation is unusual, so even though it goes against your training, please have a seat."

When the butler sank onto the settee with a sigh, Isabelle continued.

"Last night, I spoke to Lord Fagean, and he seems to think we can weather the storm. And I must say the man is an idiot. You have warned him about the staff leaving, and so have I, but he has his head in the sand, assuming nothing will change. Ask the staff to pack their clothes unobtrusively, and I will give you enough coins to pay for rooms and food at the inn. I haven't spoken to John Coachman, but tonight, before dinner, I will ask him to hitch up the dray and drive you all to the inn. Please ensure no one gets drunk and aggressive. I will notify you when the women leave and have John collect you all.'

"My Lady, how will you manage without us?"

"Ask the cook to leave a tub of water on the stove for washing, and ask a footman to set up the fireplace in my room so I will be warm if it gets cold. We will eat bread and cheese, and hopefully, their inability to fend for themselves will have those women fleeing."

Andrews laughed.

"Thank you, my lady. It's tempting to hide here to see the tantrum those women will throw."

"I assure you, their screams will probably be heard from the inn."

Once the staff left, the women's complaints immediately started as they attempted to change for dinner. No amount of shouting produced a maid to help, and their muttered complaints and punishments for the staff rang through the house. When Zavier and his sisters entered the dining room, the lack of candles and food on the table stunned them. Zavier felt a frisson of fear; where were his staff? Storming into the kitchen, he discovered Isabelle calmly sitting at the table with a loaf of bread and cheese before her.

"What in the dickens are you doing, and where the hell are the staff?"

Isabelle smiled. "Good evening, my Lord. I am eating dinner, and as promised, your staff have left. We will have to fend for ourselves. Would you like to join me? Setting up the dining room to eat bread and cheese seems ridiculous.".

Zavier spluttered, his agitation making him speechless.

"My Lord, do you not recall our conversation last night? Do you remember Andrews coming to you to inform you that the staff were looking for other employment? You have chosen to allow your sisters to stay, so the servants have left. Andrews told me that your father's death saddened the staff, but not having to deal with your sisters whenever they arrived unannounced was a relief. But the relief was short-lived because you didn't throw the nasty harpies out of the house when they arrived. You had a choice, and you made it."

Isabelle wrapped the cheese and bread in a cloth and, collecting a candle, walked away from her stunned husband. As she walked towards her room, Lady Elizabeth blocked the hallway, forcing Isabelle to stop.

"What kind of establishment do you run? Where are the servants? How are we supposed to feed ourselves without them here?"

"You could always do what I did and eat some bread and cheese. The bread is fresh, so eating it for tea is no hardship."

"No hardship! Ladies don't eat bread and cheese for their main meal. Are you mad?"

"Well, then, it appears that you will go hungry. Excuse me, I want to go to my room."

"Esme, come quickly."

The second sister arrived in the hallway, and Isabelle felt a sense of nervousness. How far would these women go, and where was her husband?

"Where are the servants? I wish to eat, and it is past dinner time."

"I was trying to spare your feelings, although God only knows if you have any. You two uninvited guests are evil harpies with the nastiest disposition of anyone I know. You are selfish and entitled, and while your brother thought to humour you, the staff gave him an ultimatum. Now he has his beloved sisters and no staff. If you realise your limitations, you might be kind to servants in future, but for now, you will have to fend for yourself, as I have no intention of waiting on you."

Isabelle pushed past the two women and retired to her bedroom.

While the servants' absence didn't affect Isabelle as badly as Zavier's sisters, there was one precaution she forgot to take. Before her maid left, Isabelle intended to change into a front-buttoning garment, but in the confusion associated with helping the staff to go, she forgot to do so. Despite twisting and turning, she could not unlace her dress, so she would have to swallow her pride and ask Zavier to help. As Isabelle walked towards her husband's bed chamber, she hoped she wouldn't come across her sisters-in-law. When she tapped on his door, there was no answer, and after repeating her knock, the Duke yanked open the door. His expression changed from murderous to confused, and Isabelle realised that her husband was at his wits' end.

"My Lord, I have a problem. Without a maid, I can't unlace the ties on my dress and rather than sleep in the garment, I hoped you would assist and unlace me."

Zavier nodded. "That I can do."

"We need to move to my room. I don't want to stand in the hallway half undressed."

Zavier escorted his wife to the guest room she inhabited.

"Why did you choose the room furthest away?"

"Because I wanted to be as far from your sisters as possible. I was angry at you for failing to see the problem, so I didn't want to be near you, either."

"I never thought it would come to this."

"Your decision to let your sisters stay didn't affect you because you spend most of the day in your study. The rest of us have endured hours and days of abuse and criticism. I have never before come across such angry harpies as those two. Anyhow, can you please unlace me?"

Isabelle turned her back and felt the pull of the laces. Zavier's warm fingers traced the laces, and Isabelle's heart rate increased. She never felt the slightest twinge of awareness with her maid, but the presence of her husband set her nerves alight. Zavier pushed the dress from her shoulders as it loosened around her. Isabelle went to move away, but her husband's voice stopped her.

"Don't you want me to help undo your stays?"

Isabelle blushed.

"Certainly, my Lord."

Isabelle felt her husband's lips on her neck as her stays loosened. As she stood in her chemise, Zavier's lips made a slow and lazy exploration of her neck and shoulders. Isabelle shivered; the feeling of his lips made her stomach flutter and her heartbeat race. Isabelle knew she should stop Zavier's advances, but from their first meeting, she wondered what it would feel like to have him kiss her. As Zavier turned her, Isabelle's breath hitched, and when he cupped her cheek with his hand, she thought she would swoon.

Someone shouting his name broke the moment, and Zavier swore under his breath. He dipped his head and kissed Isabelle lightly before leaving the bedroom. Stunned by what had happened and the speed with which Zavier left her room, Isabelle felt dazed. She collected the discarded clothes and locked the door. When she and Zavier finally consummated their marriage, she didn't want her sisters-in-law in the house.

Isabelle lay in bed, replaying Zavier's kisses. She knew she should sleep; tomorrow would be as trying as this afternoon without servants to wait on Zavier's sisters, but the giddy feeling Zavier made her feel was hard to quell.

Chapter Fifteen

The following day was as tough as Isabelle predicted. She rose early and, after coaxing the banked coals to light the wood, she added to the fire, cooked eggs and toast. Isabelle felt a sense of satisfaction at the meal she cooked. It might have been a simple meal, but one that would sustain them throughout the day. When Lady Esme and Lady Elisabeth viewed the offerings for their breakfast, they were aghast. They loudly complained about the food offered for breakfast, and Isabelle wondered how long her husband would prefer the company of his sisters to the comfort provided by the servants. The sisters were further outraged that Isabelle dished their meal in the kitchen instead of them dining in the breakfast room.

"Zavier, this is outrageous! How could you allow your wife to serve us such a poor breakfast in the kitchen?"

Isabelle spoke before Zavier could respond.

"Ladies, if your cooking skills extend further than mine, I'm certain neither Zavier nor I would stop you from preparing a lavish meal for us."

Zavier looked up from his plate.

"Esme and Elizabeth, you seem to forget that the simple meal is your fault. If you hadn't chased off the servants with your nasty temper and constant criticism, Isabelle wouldn't need to be preparing food. And I, for one, am pleased Isabelle could cook our meal; otherwise, we would have to eat bread and cheese. After breakfast, I suggest you pack your trunks, and I will notify your driver that you will be ready to leave by lunchtime. If you spend the night in an inn, you can hire their private dining room and eat a hearty meal."

Zavier watched his sisters' stunned faces as he rose, and their outraged expressions nearly made him laugh. He approached Isabelle, and his eyes skimmed over her face.

"Thank you, my lady, for preparing our meal."

Turning back to his sisters, he said, "Oh, and by the way, Esme and Elizabeth, you will not arrive unannounced for a visit ever again. In fact, after this debacle, you will not visit at all."

As Lord Fagean left the kitchen, his sisters directed their anger and outrage at Isabelle. When they ran out of offensive comments, Isabelle rose from her seat.

"Your insults don't affect me now that I know you will be gone by lunchtime. The joy of never seeing you again gladdens my heart. You'll forgive me if I don't see you off; you are the most hateful women I have ever met, and I am happy that my husband has finally evicted you. My sympathy goes out to your husbands. How they manage to live with you is a mystery, or maybe they spend their days in their offices and their nights in their mistress's beds."

Their shrieks of outrage left Isabelle unmoved. Leaving the two disgruntled women in the kitchen, Isabelle felt such joy that she skipped along the hallway to her room. She grinned as she considered the difficulty the women would have packing their trunks. The sisters would discover that packing their cases was not a skill they excelled at, and the absence of the maids would hit even harder than it had the night before. In preparation for the servants' return, Isabelle penned a note to Andrews and walked to the stable to ask one of the grooms to deliver the message. She also notified John Coachman that once the carriage carrying Lady Esme and Lady Elizabeth left the estate, he could prepare the dray to collect the servants.

The evening meal was a welcome change from cheese and bread, and Isabelle asked Andrews to thank the cook for her efforts. As she and Zavier chatted while they dined, the topic turned to his sister's behaviour.

"Why are your sisters so angry? I've never come across such entitled, horrid women in my life. I understand that living on the continent alone must have caused you stress, but I'm not sure you'd have been happier living with them."

Zavier sighed. "I don't know what has made them angry. When I took over the estate, they arrived unannounced, but I thought nothing of it, assuming they had come to help get the place in order. If they abused the staff, I didn't notice because the mess my father left took all of my concentration."

"Believe me, my lord; they certainly abused the staff. Even while your father was alive, they caused problems."

"Thankfully, they've gone, and we shouldn't have any more visits from them. Will you move bedrooms now that they are gone?"

"I'll ask Mrs Hopkins to help me complete the renovations in your mother's room before I move. It shouldn't take more than a day or two, and then I'll move my things. Once we finish that, I will get the footmen to help move all the rooms' carpets and swap them around. I'll probably change the quilts, so if we are ever foolish enough to invite your sisters to stay, their bedrooms as they remember them, will be gone."

Zavier laughed."I knew you were feisty from the moment I met you. My appearance stunned your mother, but you took control of the social niceties despite your mother's objections."

After a moment's silence, Zavier shook his head and looked Isabelle in the face.

"I'm sorry. What I did to you was unforgivable. I was so filled with hate and desperately wanted to pay your mother for all the years I was exiled that I lost my objectivity. I doubted that I could discredit her, so I foolishly thought the only way to pay her back was through you. After spending that first ride together, I questioned my actions, but then she stuck her nose in again, and I pushed my misgivings aside. I told Gareth that if your mother were anyone else, I would offer for you because I liked you, but my course of action ruined any chance I had with you. Gareth told me he suggested offering for you, and the thought of you on someone else's arm turned my stomach. And when I imagined you growing big with some other man's babe, I knew I had to offer for you. I'm so glad that your father saw the sense of the union, but I'm sorry we forced you to marry me."

Zavier's apology stunned Isabelle, and for the first time since their wedding, she felt they might make a go of this marriage.

"Thank you, my lord. I'm glad you and my father tricked me into this marriage; otherwise, I would be scrubbing floors on my hands and knees."

Zavier laughed as he turned and headed for his bedroom.

Isabelle watched her husband leave and wondered if there was a message behind his inquiry regarding her sleeping arrangements. After so many weeks, did he intend to consummate the marriage, or was his question merely a matter of curiosity? Although Isabelle wasn't sure what happened between a man and a woman in the bedroom, she felt confident that Zavier could train her to please a man after the reports of his rakish ways in his youth. Did Zavier have a mistress? While he courted her, she had seen no suggestion of another woman, but his disappearance after their argument raised the question: where did he go, and who did he visit? Isabelle knew other women found him attractive, but she didn't intend to be a wife in name only while her husband rushed off to see his mistress. Perhaps this was a discussion they needed before their relationship could develop further.

As Isabelle walked towards her bedroom, she felt a wave of loneliness swamp her. She had moved to the end of the hall to avoid Zavier's sisters, but now the problems and noise they caused were gone; she felt the solitude of her bedchamber.

Chapter Sixteen

Isabelle sighed with satisfaction as she gazed around her room. The walls were a pale shade of lemon, and the curtains and duvet had traces of yellow in their floral design. There was no sign of the destruction caused by her dead father-in-law, and she had banished the ghost of her mother-in-law. Now that she occupied the bedchamber that adjoined her husband's room, Isabelle wondered if he might come to her tonight. Did she have to offer him an invitation, or would he take it upon himself to visit without being asked? Isabelle realised there were so many questions she should have asked her mother. Still, Lady Hazel Beaumont disapproved of the union her husband had organised, so Isabelle doubted that she would answer her questions honestly. Would her mother admit her responsibility in Zavier's exile, or would she firmly hold onto the belief that it was his fault for not offering for her? Isabelle was thankful that Zavier hadn't bedded her mother; the thought that she could have married a man who knew her mother intimately made her feel ill.

The day was drawing to a close when Isabelle decided to retire for the night. Once her maid had braided her hair and helped her into her night rail, Isabelle dismissed the girl and climbed into bed. The murmur of male voices from the next room indicated that Zavier was preparing for bed with his valet's assistance. Isabelle listened to their voices, comforted by the fact that she was no longer alone. As she prepared to snuff out the candle on the bedside cabinet, the door to Zavier's room opened, and he entered. Isabelle watched as he stalked across the room, and her heartbeat stuttered when he sat beside her. The smirk that crossed his face made her feel like swooning, and she was glad she was seated; otherwise, she might have collapsed from the effect his proximity had on her.

"My Lord, what brings you to my bedchamber?"

"Isabelle, we need to talk."

His words dashed Isabelle's hopes, but she was determined that he wouldn't see disappointment on her face.

"If you wished to discuss something, why didn't you raise the issue over dinner?"

Zavier grinned. "I don't think Andrews and the other servers wanted to be privy to our bedroom arrangements."

Isabelle blushed. "Very well, my lord, please proceed with your conversation."

Zavier took Isabelle's hand and said, "I am getting on in age and need an heir. To get an heir, I need to bed you. Do you know what happens between a man and a woman?"

Isabelle's voice was so shaky that she had to clear her throat to answer his question.

"No."

Zavier sighed. "Why would I ever imagine that your mother would get off her high horse and instruct you on your duties as a wife?"

"My Lord, do you have a mistress?"

Zavier raised his eyebrows at the change of direction the conversation had taken.

"No, why do you ask?"

"Where did you go when you disappeared?"

"You want to talk about this now?"

Isabelle nodded. "Yes."

"I told your father I could talk you around, but when you refused to talk to me, and we argued, I started to doubt myself. The thought of years of silence and recriminations wasn't appealing. A hunting lodge is at the back of the property, and I holed up there for several days. After wallowing and feeling sorry for myself, I returned, intent on talking to you, but my sisters were here. After that, there was no opportunity to discuss our marriage."

"Thank you. So, back to the subject of begetting an heir."

Zavier ran his hand through his previously neat hair and said, "There are two ways to approach the bedding. The fast way is the method many men married to ladies take, but there is little joy in that method, which is why so many husbands have mistresses."

"For the fast way, what would I have to do?"

"Close your eyes, open your legs and let me get on with it. It can be quite painful for the woman, so they lie there praying their husbands will quickly finish."

Isabelle's mouth opened, but no sound came out. Dear God, what had she let herself in for? Zavier watched the expressions flit across her face; she was as easy to read as a book.

"There is an alternative. Would you like me to tell you about that?"

Isabelle nodded mutely.

"This bedding takes longer, but if we use the slower method, I can make the experience enjoyable for us both. You must trust me to take care of you, and if I do something you don't like, you must tell me."

"Will it still hurt?"

"There might be a moment of pain the first time because I assume you are a maiden. But after that, it won't hurt."

"I don't want you to have a mistress, so if the slow way will stop that and you say it is enjoyable, it would be best if we take the second choice."

"Then, my sweet, come over here."

Isabelle slid closer to Zavier, and he tilted her head to feast on her neck. He shifted his focus from her neck to her mouth when she was writhing and panting. Nobody had ever kissed Isabelle before, but with his encouragement, they moved past closed-mouth kisses to explore each other's mouths. Isabelle was so focused on what Zavier was doing with his mouth that he had pushed her nightrail to her waist and bared her breasts before she realised. When Zavier fondled her breasts and licked them, Isabelle squirmed and wriggled. Her gasps and groans urged him on, and Zavier thanked the lord that she hadn't chosen the fast method many ladies preferred.

He heard her gasp when he trailed his hands between her legs, but he soothed her with sounds and quiet words, and she relaxed into his touch. Her reluctance vanished when he circled her clit with his fingers wet from her folds. As Isabelle ground against him, he watched her face, flushed with arousal. He grinned when she stiffened and yelled his name; his proper little wife was a passionate bedmate. As Isabelle groaned, Zavier dropped his pants and levered himself over her. Isabelle's eyes flew open when he entered her in slow increments.

"Relax, sweetheart, or this won't go as well."

Zavier leaned over and kissed her, and he felt her muscles relax as she became distracted by his kiss. When he breached her maidenhead, she yanked her head away from him and squealed. With tears in her eyes, she accused, "You said it wouldn't hurt."

"Lie still a moment, and the pain will go."

He knew when the pain receded because Isabelle began to wriggle and writhe. Taking that as his sign that she was ready to continue, he moved, picking up a steady rhythm.

"Wrap your legs around me."

Isabelle's brain didn't work; she followed her husband's instructions as he drove her to ecstasy. When his body stiffened, and he let out a shout, she opened her eyes to watch in amazement at the expression on his face.

"Ah, Izzy, you kill me."

She hoped that was a good thing, and when he cleaned her with a damp cloth and curled up against her in bed, she thought it might be.

Chapter Seventeen

Isabelle wore the contented look of a satisfied woman. Zavier loved that he could put that look on her face, and he also enjoyed her enthusiasm for the task of begetting an heir. His belief that he could talk her around when they first married had now come to pass, and Isabelle and Zavier were blissfully happy. The servants who had witnessed the messy start to their employers' marriage settled into their tasks with gratitude that the need to abandon the estate would not happen again. After years of harassment and bad-tempered comments, the staff heaved a sigh of relief that the Duke had banned his hateful sisters from visiting.

"I have to visit the other properties my family owns."

The comment Zavier made came out of the blue, and Isabelle felt like pouting. Why, when everything was going well, did Zavier have to leave? She knew that Zavier's family owned other properties, and after setting things up at their primary estate, he needed to see how the stewards managed the different properties.

"Can I accompany you?"

Zavier shook his head. "No, the outriders and I will move quickly, and a carriage will slow us down."

Isabelle's happy face disappeared, and her brow wrinkled in frustration.

"Will you be gone for long?"

"If all is well with the other three properties, I should be gone for a week."

"And if all is not well?"

Zavier groaned. "If the properties are as run-down as this estate was when I returned, I could be there for weeks. If that happens, I will send a message for you to join me."

Isabelle sighed. She understood the need to oversee the unentailed properties, but regretted that their newfound happiness would be interrupted.

After Zavier's departure, Isabelle missed her husband. Still, she was not one to sulk, so she spent her time sorting the myriad of discarded and forgotten objects in the attic. While Mrs Hopkins fretted about the dust and grime in the attic, Isabelle would not allow her housekeeper's disapproval to sway her. Time had ruined many of the stored items, and many were beyond repair, but occasionally, Isabelle found a gem that someone had placed there many years ago and had forgotten. She was investigating a similar find when Mrs Hopkins entered the room.

"Lady Isabelle, the Duke's sisters have arrived. Thank the Lord, they don't have trunks with them, but they insist on speaking to you."

Isabelle pulled a face. "Whatever those harpies have to say is sure to ruin my day. Did Andrews let them into the house?"

"Yes. Andrews could see they didn't have trunks on the carriage, so he thought he should allow them entry. He has placed them in the sitting room. Should I order refreshments while Ruthie helps you tidy up?"

Isabelle shook her head. "No. I want those women out of my home as soon as possible, and we won't delay their departure by pretending this is a welcome visit."

Once Isabelle washed her hands and face, Ruthie unravelled the braids in Isabelle's hair and helped her adorn a plain house dress. As she left the bedroom, she grinned at her maid and said, "Wish me luck."

Entering the sitting room, Isabelle made no pretence of pleasure at seeing the women, and her greeting was brief.

"After Zavier evicted you from our home, I didn't expect to see you again. What brings you here?"

Lady Esme rose and approached Isabelle.

"We have unfinished business. The local gossip is that Zavier is away from the estate for a week, so we decided to take advantage of his absence to deal with you."

Isabelle stepped back. The woman had a mad gleam in her eye, and Isabelle suddenly felt fearful. When Lady Elizabeth joined her sister to present a united front, Isabelle knew it was time to call Andrews to remove the women. Before she could call her butler, Lady Esme pulled a snub-nosed gun from her reticule and pointed it at Isabelle.

"If you value your butler's life, you will not alert him to our plot. You will smile as we walk to the carriage and convince him all is well, or I will shoot the man. The magistrate won't care if the world has one less servant, particularly when I accuse him of manhandling me. Now, move!"

Isabelle was no match for the two women, and fear for Andrews's life prevented her from calling for help. All too soon, Isabelle was in the carriage as it sped away from the estate. Elizabeth produced a length of rope, and she tied Isabelle's hands together. Despite Isabelle's vulnerability, Lady Esme kept the gun trained on her captive.

"Why are you doing this? Zavier will come looking for me, and you two will end up in jail."

While Esme looked smug and grinned at Isabelle, Elizabeth seemed less confident. If Esme left the coach for any reason, Isabelle thought she might sway Elizabeth to her cause. Isabelle's plan came to naught when the carriage drove through the night after a short stop to change the horses. With the increased traffic, the driver slowed the carriage, and Isabelle wondered if she could fling herself from the vehicle, but with the gun still pointed at her, she doubted her ability to open the door and flee. The sounds and smell alerted Isabelle to their arrival in town; Esme ordered her out of the carriage shortly after. The building before the women was grim and foreboding, with bars on the windows and a guard at the gate, giving Isabelle the shivers.

"What is this place?"

Elizabeth smiled. "It's the debtors' prison. Zavier will never find you, and we intend to tell him you begged us to help you escape."

Esme and Elizabeth pushed Isabelle before them as they entered the building. A guard approached, and Esme said,

"This is the woman we spoke to the governor about, and he said he could accommodate her."

The guard nodded. "Bring her through here. I will put her in with the other toffs who can't pay their bills."

Isabelle grabbed the man's arm. "Please wait. I am Lady Isabelle Fagean, and my husband is the Duke of Kenmore. I am not destitute and have no trouble paying my debts."

"That's what they all say, and your sisters-in-law assure me that your husband no longer wants you, so there is no way you can pay your debts. The governor showed me some of the demands from merchants, so you can't wriggle out of this." The man scoffed and dragged Isabelle forward.

As the gate clanged behind her, Isabelle heard her sister-in-law laugh. "Have a wonderful life, Isabelle. You can rest assured, we will be making unannounced visits. Zavier will allow us free rein at the estate now that he doesn't have to appease you."

The tears that Isabelle had held at bay during the carriage ride spilled over, and she wept. A hand on her shoulder startled her, and she turned to see a group of women behind her.

"The tears don't help, my dear. Our husbands have deserted us by dying and leaving nothing in place for our futures or by finding a more affluent, younger candidate. If your husband loves you, as you say, he will have trouble locating you because this is not a place most people are familiar with. The best you can do is try to stay sane."

Looking at the six other women in the cell, Isabelle could see that those years of despair had ravaged what had once been attractive women. Would she look like them once it became apparent that Zavier was not searching for her?

Chapter Eighteen

Andrews was beside himself. He didn't buy the excuse that Isabelle was accompanying her sisters-in-law to visit her new nieces and nephews. Sending riders to stop the coach was not something he could do. Besides, most of the outriders had accompanied the Duke. Andrews knew of the unentailed properties, but sending messengers to three country estates could take days before the letters arrived. As he wrung his hands, he cursed the sisters who had been the bane of his life for so long.

Three days later, when a message arrived for the Duchess, Andrews made an executive decision and opened the document. He blushed as he read the note, but the Duke's request that Lady Isabelle join him at Childers allowed Andrews to alert Lord Fagean of his concerns. Andrews dispatched a messenger with the instruction to deliver his missive post haste. Three days after the messenger left, Lord Fagean arrived, exhausted, dishevelled and angry. After shedding his coat, Zavier called for Brandy and the butler.

"Andrews, what the dickens happened? What the devil is this rot about Isabelle visiting my nieces and nephews?"

Andrews, who was usually stoic and prided himself on his lack of facial expressions when dealing with his betters, wrung his hands like an elderly matron.

"My Lord, your sisters arrived, and because they had no trunks, I allowed them entry. Lady Isabelle met them in the sitting room, and the women left together. Your sisters were smiling broadly, but although she said everything was all right, Lady Isabelle looked like she was trying to hide her tears. We haven't seen her since. I wasn't sure where you were until your message arrived for Lady Isabelle. I regret to inform you that I opened the letter and read it to ascertain your location."

Zavier didn't bat an eyelid as the butler announced he had read the private note to his wife.

"Get the footmen to draw a bath, tell Mrs Hopkins I need a meal, and I will nap before heading off in search of my wife. Tell the outriders we leave again just before dark, and we'll make as much distance as possible before stopping at an inn once night falls. And tell them to be armed."

As Zavier bathed, he fretted about what his sisters wanted with his wife. Isabelle was feisty but not able to defend herself against two strong women. Zavier cursed himself for ever letting the women into the house, and he vowed that if any harm came to Isabelle, he'd see them both on a slow boat to one of the new colonies.

The sun was dipping low in the sky as Zavier and his outriders left the estate. Zavier kept the riders at a steady pace, aware that they had a long ride ahead of them. During his meal, he decided to visit Elizabeth's house first; she was far easier to bluff than Esme. If he were to locate Isabelle, he needed one of the sisters to confess. Cursing the coming dark and the lack of a moon tonight, Zavier and his men took lodgings at a small inn they came across. After a meal, the men retired, but Zavier spent hours pacing the floor, grieving his wife's loss. Finally succumbing to fatigue, he conceded that he could do nothing to help Isabelle in the dark of the night.

The house belonging to his sister, Elizabeth, and her husband, Henry, came into view as they topped the rise. Looking at the perfect gardens and the tranquil setting made Zavier's temper spike. Why couldn't his sister be happy with the regal manor house and the peaceful setting? When the grooms ran out to collect their horses, Zavier and his men approached the front door. The expression on the butler's face was one of abject horror when confronted by seven burly men.

"Lord Zavier Ragean to see Lady Elizabeth,"

With trepidation, the butler allowed the men to enter and scurried off with his message for his mistress. It didn't surprise Zavier when the butler announced that his mistress was not accepting visitors. Controlling his temper, Zavier said, " And what of Lord Blackmore? Is he available?"

"I'll enquire."

The posse of men in his foyer startled Henry Blackmore.

"Lord Fagaen, I assume you are not making a social call. Send your men to the kitchen, and we can discuss the trouble that brought you here. Edmond, ask Mrs Fich to send some refreshments to the sitting room."

Henry said when the men were seated, "I assume this visit is about my wife and her sister's last visit. It was hard to follow the tale of deserting servants, but maybe you could explain that in more detail."

"Yes, this is about my sisters' last visit, but it is more recent than you might imagine. Your wife and her sister arrived at my estate five or six days ago. I was away on business, but they said they wanted to talk to Isabelle. My butler said that while the three women walked out to the carriage, Isabelle was pale and on the verge of tears. I want to know where the hell my wife is, and knowing my sisters, I am more likely to get an answer from Elizabeth than Esme."

Henry strode to the door.

"Edmond, send my wife to the sitting room."

A knock on the door revealed the butler's anxious face.

"My lord, she said she has a migraine and regrets she cannot visit with her brother."

Henry strode out into the hallway and ascended the stairs swiftly.

"Elizabeth, I will send your maid to help you dress, but if you aren't in the sitting room in ten minutes, I will drag you out in whatever attire you are wearing."

Returning to the sitting room, Henry poured the tea and offered Zavier some pastries.

"Tell me what happened during the visit when you evicted your sisters."

Despite being edgy and angry, Zavier related the details of the sister's visit. A moment or two later, Elizabeth walked into the room.

"Ah, my dear, you look remarkably well for a lady with a debilitating headache. Your brother has questions for you, and I'd advise you to consider your answers."

Zavier looked at his sister with disgust. "What did you do to Isabelle? Where is she?"

"I didn't do anything to Isabelle."

"She is missing and was last seen with you and Esme."

Elizabeth sat on the settee, wringing her handkerchief in her fingers.

Zavier rose and shouted, "Damn you, Elizabeth, where is she?"

Elizabeth gave her husband a pitiful look. "Are you going to let him bully me?"

"My dear, until you give him a truthful answer, her can yell all he likes."

"It was Esme's idea. If we got rid of Isabelle, we could visit the estate whenever we wanted. We didn't think you liked her much, or you didn't seem to when we were there, so we didn't think you would care." Elizabeth began to weep.

"If you tell me you sold her to a slaver or killed her, I will see you hang, little sister. Tell me where she is."

"We left her at the Winchester debtors' prison."

Zavier sprang from his seat. Henry followed closely behind.

"I will organise the driver to take the coach to the prison, but I will ride with you. I will deal with my wife later."

Zavier yelled for his men, and they hurried from the kitchen.

" She is at the Winchester debtors' prison. Mount up; we are leaving now."

As Henry yelled instructions to his driver, the men mounted, and within minutes, they headed towards Winchester at a fast clip.

Chapter Nineteen

The façade of the old building filled Zavier with fear. How could the authorities believe this grim-looking building should house people just because they were poor? The guard at the gate attempted to prevent Zavier, Henry and their men from entering.

"Who is in charge here?"

When Zavier pulled him up by the neck of his shirt, the man's eyes looked like they would pop out of his head.

"Where is the governor?"

The man pointed behind him, and Zavier dropped him to the ground as the men strode along the path.

"Brother-in-law, try a little subtly with the head guy. You might get a better response."

Zavier grunted as he continued along the path. He pushed open a large door, and a man sat behind an enormous mahogany desk. A colourful carpet covered the stone floors, and tapestries and hangings adorned the walls. Despite the rundown exterior, this man certainly did not lack anything. The man raised his eyes from the document he was perusing and scowled at the men standing in his office.

"What is the meaning of this?"

Henry spoke first, "Let me introduce myself. I am Lord Henry Blackmore, Earl of Hustonville County, and this is my brother-in-law, Lord Zavier Fagaen, Duke of Kenmore. We believe you have erroneously jailed Lady Isabelle, Fagean's wife, and we wish to retrieve her."

The man blustered about always following the rule book and having paperwork to back up the claims; it was improbable that Lady Isabelle was in his prison.

"If you don't know where my wife is, we will unlock every cell until we find her."

The man huffed. "If she is here, she will be in the toff's cells. We try to keep the swells away from the common folk."

Doing his best to keep his temper under control, Zavier said, "Would you escort us to the section of the jail where you keep the toffs, as you call them?"

The governor complained about the interruption to his day, and Henry spoke before Zavier completely lost his temper.

"Sir, we understand that you don't wish to leave your guilded office to mix with the poor folk you have locked in your jail, but if you don't escort us, we will do as my brother-in-law said and open every cell until we find Lady Isabelle.

And I don't believe the magistrate will listen to your complaints when Lord Fagean explains why he beat you to a pulp."

The man's face paled, and he heaved his bulk from his chair. Zavier wondered how an officer of the crown could be so obese and feared that the food destined for the cells never reached them. As they followed the man, Zavier was appalled at the condition of the people he passed. Skeletal hands came out of the cells, and the eyes of the inmates were wild and haunted. Zavier vowed that once he retrieved Isabelle, he would complain to the judiciary about the treatment of these poor blighters. Poor or not, people should never be treated worse than the animals in the fields.

When the governor stopped at a cell, he said, "Well, Lord Fagean, which one of these women is your wife?"

Zavier looked over the women, and Isabelle was not amongst the sad faces he could see.

"Damnation, why is she not here if your wife said she was?

Could she have been placed in another cell by mistake?"

A woman presented herself at the cell door.

"Who are you looking for, my Lord?"

"My wife, Lady Isabelle Fagean."

"One moment, please."

The woman walked to a pallet in the far corner and shook its inhabitant.

"Isabelle, your husband is here."

The pile of clothes on the bed shifted, and Zavier nearly cried with relief when Isabelle's dirty face emerged from the heap.

"Zavier?"

Zavier glared at the jailer. "Open the damn door."

"Well, there is a slight problem. Lady Isabelle must have unpaid debts, and I can't release her without payment of that money."

Henry held Zavier back as he surged forward to punch the man.

"I have a solution. Why don't you and I return to your office to discuss the repayments, and while we do that, you could get your assistant to release Isabelle?"

Henry led the head governor away while the other man opened the cell. Isabelle walked towards her husband, but her restraint fractured as she got closer, and she threw herself into his arms.

"I was so scared you wouldn't find me, and I'd have to stay here forever."

Zavier wrapped his arms around his wife and thanked God that Elizabeth had confessed before too many more days passed.

When Henry and the jailer returned, the man looked well satisfied, and Henry motioned to the assistant.

"Open the cell door. I have paid the debts for these six ladies, and they will be coming with us."

Amazed silence greeted Henry's announcement, and then the women wept with gratitude. As the women filed out of the cell, Isabelle stepped out of Zavier's embrace and said, "Please, my lord, can we release Franny and her children? The boy turns ten in a week, and the jailer will move him to the men's prison. A ten-year-old amongst all those men does not bode well for his safety."

Henry shook his head in disgust. He handed the jailer and his assistant some coins and motioned for the man to release the woman and her two children.

Henry surveyed the women and said, "Zavier, why don't you all stay overnight? You can use my carriage and yours to transport the women. What are your plans?"

Zavier ran his fingers through his hair and said, " The ladies can live in the dower house until they are well and we make some solid plans."

Zavier sent two of his outriders to intercept his carriage and direct his driver to meet them at Lord Blacknmore's estate, but for now, Henry's carriage and a hired hack would do the job.

As Zavier sat with Henry after the women settled for the night, he realised that losing Isabelle would be worse than living in exile for most of his life. How the bubbly, outspoken chit had captured his heart was a mystery, although in truth, when he put his revenge plan into action, he never imagined that he would develop feelings for her. Seeing her today in the filth and squalor of the prison was not a memory that would disappear in a hurry. His sisters' hatred of the woman he married was unbearable, and he knew that Henry would punish his wife; however, the main perpetrator, Esme, was unaware of the rescue. He decided to take a detour before he and Isabelle headed home.

Rising to take his leave, Zavier said, "I'm ready to retire, but thank you for your assistance in rescuing Isabelle and the other women."

Henry nodded. "It was the least I could do. My wife might need a stint in the country, and I will prohibit her from associating with her sister. The woman is a menace, and if being separated from her makes Elizabeth more settled, then I will be grateful."

Zavier entered the bedroom quietly, unwilling to disturb Isabelle, but he needed the comfort of her body curled against him. When he slipped into bed, Isabelle slid towards him, and he settled to sleep with his arm wrapped around her. Zavier listened to the steady rhythm of Isabelle's breathing, and contentment flowed over him. For the first time in his life, he felt wanted, and after years of exile and loneliness, the feeling was exquisite. This little slip of a girl had captured his heart, and while he still felt angry at what his sisters had done, the comfort of his bed and his wife helped mute his anger. Tomorrow would be soon enough to vent his anger. That was the last thought he had before sleep overtook him.

Epilogue

After months of sending messages back and forth, the ladies rescued from the debtors' prison travelled across the sea to make new lives in America. The colony had transformed from the wild frontier that marked its inception, and now its inhabitants were a more diverse range of people, many of whom were men. Female companionship and prospective wives were in short supply, so many men resorted to applying for mail-order brides. Two of the older rescues, not interested in becoming wives, had ventured across the sea to set up a mail-order bride agency. With Zavier's financial backing, the women vetted the applications and sent letters from the men to the ladies at the Fagean estate. As the last ladies left the estate, Isabelle tossed up the wisdom of speaking to Zavier about an idea that plagued her mind. Over dinner that night, she decided that if Zavier quashed her suggestion, she would abandon her plan for now.

"Zavier, now the ladies are gone; I thought about helping those poor people in the prison."

Zavier glanced up from his meal and looked at his wife.

"I'm not sure what more we can do. Henry and I approached the governor and described the prison conditions and the excesses in the headman's office. We also suggested that while that blighter was grossly overweight, the residents were starving, so it wasn't hard to guess where the bulk of the food went. What more do you think we can do?"

"With much ado, we managed to secure new lives in America for seven ladies. Why can't we place more women in the new colony? There are widows and single women in prison, and there are women like me whom society considers ruined. Surely we can offer some of those women a better life? There is nothing we can do for married ladies unless their husbands are imprisoned for crimes other than failure to pay debts; then, they would have to want to divorce their husbands. However, the others should be no more difficult to place than the ladies who have already left. After spending only a few days there, I felt the despair and hopelessness that every other resident suffers. I can't for the life of me imagine what those women feel after years of imprisonment."

Zavier raised his eyebrows. "And in your condition, you are prepared to help more women? You know, there might be an endless number of women in dire straits. We can't send them all to America."

"My condition does not make me incapable of helping. You are correct that we can't send all the women to America, but even if they don't want to marry, they can become shopkeepers or seamstresses. We can offer them hope and a better future. This country has such riches that no one should go hungry or go to jail for being poor."

Zavier nodded. "I will send a message to Henry, and we will approach the governor with your scheme. I can't imagine the man disagreeing because the overheads at the prison pull on the government's purse strings. But I insist that you find an assistant to help you implement your plan; I'll not have you tiring yourself."

Isabelle smiled. "Thank you, my lord. Knowing that the dower house operates as a halfway house would horrify your parents and grandparents. I will find a helper as soon as the next group of women join us. We should consult with the society matrons to determine if any debutantes or women considered ruined live in exile on country estates. They will have to be open to living without servants and doing for themselves, so we may get no girls open to my plan, but we'll see."

Once the new residents arrived, Isabelle began to feel weighed down by her increasing weight. She hoped to have the new rescues situated before her baby's arrival, but time was running out. One of the older women, whom Isabelle had rescued, became her assistant and took over most of the organising, allowing Isabelle to step back. Working on feedback from her American-based mail-order office, Isabelle set the cook the task of teaching the women to cook. Some women responsible for preparing the food for their families could cook, but many had no skills. Isabelle was determined that the women she sent as brides would be an asset to their husbands. Any woman intent on setting up businesses still needed the ability to feed themselves.

Zavier watched as Isabelle stepped back from the organising and knew her time was near. While he was excited at the imminent arrival of an offspring, worry niggled at his brain. The thought of his wife suffering through childbirth turned his blood cold. Didn't women die giving birth? Zavier knew he could do nothing to help, but he was responsible for her predicament. If this child were a boy, could he refrain from being intimate with Isabelle to save her the pain of another birth? He didn't think he had that much self-control, but he could practise over the months and years ahead. The thought was sobering.

When Isabelle arrived at the house earlier than he expected, the bevy of women accompanying her made it clear that her time had come. Mrs Hopkins took control, shunting the women out of Isabelle's room and sending a footman for the midwife. Zavier was frozen to the spot as Mrs Hopkins ordered the maids to bring in basins of hot water, towels and the bale of twine he had secured for her only days before. Isabelle's lady's maid carried a large piece of cardboard, and Zavier thought Mrs Hopkins might use it to protect the pallet underneath. The pacing seemed pointless, but he found that sitting was torturous. What could he do? What did men do while their wives gave birth?

The groaning coming from Isabelle's bed chamber made Zavier cringe. When Andrews arrived in the hallway, Zavier barely spared him a glance.

"Your Grace, I thought this might help."

The butler handed Zavier a large goblet filled to the brim with whisky. After taking a gulp, Zavier laughed.

"Is this what men do while their women are giving birth?"

"Yes, although I always think the women could do with a slug of whisky as they toil away."

A scream tore the air, and Zavier jumped.

"Damnation!" Putting down the drink, he opened the door to Isabelle's room. The shocked look on the face of the midwife did nothing to deter Zavier's resolve to comfort Isabelle.

"Your grace, you can't be in here."

"I helped her get with child, and it's only right I help her now."

Walking to the head of the bed, Zavier clasped Isabelle's hand. The smile she gave him made the midwife's outrage pale into insignificance.

"Ruthie, get me a damp cloth for your mistress's forehead."

Two hours later, Zavier wondered how long his wife could endure this pain. The midwife, who had long forgotten his presence, said, "One more push, Lady Isabelle. It will only take one more push."

The grimace on Isabelle's face made him hope the woman was right. The worst was over when her face calmed, and the women in the room grinned. In her arms, the midwife held a squalling baby, no bigger than a skun rabbit, but this baby was a combination of Isabelle and him.

"Congratulations. Lord Fagean, you have a bonny boy."

"Thank the Lord. We won't be doing that again. My little man, you had better shape up because you will be an only child."

Isabelle opened her eyes.

"We'll see about that, my lord. For now, one is the perfect number."

Eight months after Zavier rescued her and the other society ladies, baby William Zavier Fagean was born. Zavier chuckled to himself. He had set out to ruin Isabelle, and she had claimed his heart. He decided that his happy marriage and the birth of his son were the best revenge he could inflict on Lady Beaumont.

Also by Robyn C Rye

Farnsworth Sisters
Marrying a Rogue
Rescuing Hannah

The Buckingham Sisters
Lady Maggie's Challenge
Layla's Unwanted Husband

The Evans Family
Sometimes Love is not Enough
Still the One
Moving Forward

Standalone
One More Chance
Lady Jayne's Reputation
Third Time's the Charm
Can't Stop Loving You

The Marriage Scam
An Unlikely Match
Searching For You
The Unexpected Suitor
The Lady and the Duke
Starting Over
An Unforgettable Stranger
The Duke's Revenge
The Temporary Wife
Against The Odds
Betrayed
No Good Turn Goes Unpunished
Lady Eloise's Soldier
Lillian's Forbidden Beau
Remember Me
Always Second Best
When One Door Closes
Coming Home to You
Chasing Shadows
Fool Me Once
Deserting Lady Audrey
My Unlikely Saviour
Lies and Deception
A New Beginning
Julia's Second Chance
The Hidden Enemy
The Maiden's Redemption